THE STAKE IS GOLD

by

Jinx Barnum

Dear Reader,
The story you are about to read in no way involves real people. I will admit that "Doc" has
some of Stan's characteristics but never did he lose a friend to murder or become involved in
such an investigation. All of the characters and their antics are figments of my imagination.
In no way do they mirror any specific person, place, or event.

Order this book online at www.trafford.com/07-2292
or email orders@trafford.com

Most Trafford titles are also available at major online book retailers.

Note for Librarians: A cataloguing record for this book is available from Library
and Archives Canada at www.collectionscanada.ca/amicus/index-e.html

Printed in Victoria, BC, Canada.

ISBN: 978-1-4251-5221-5

We at Trafford believe that it is the responsibility of us all, as both individuals
and corporations, to make choices that are environmentally and socially sound.
You, in turn, are supporting this responsible conduct each time you purchase a
Trafford book, or make use of our publishing services. To find out how you are
helping, please visit www.trafford.com/responsiblepublishing.html

Our mission is to efficiently provide the world's finest, most comprehensive
book publishing service, enabling every author to experience success.
To find out how to publish your book, your way, and have it available
worldwide, visit us online at www.trafford.com/10510

 www.trafford.com

North America & international
toll-free: 1 888 232 4444 (USA & Canada)
phone: 250 383 6864 ♦ fax: 250 383 6804 ♦ email: info@trafford.com

The United Kingdom & Europe
phone: +44 (0)1865 487 395 ♦ local rate: 0845 230 9601
facsimile: +44 (0)1865 481 507 ♦ email: info.uk@trafford.com

10 9 8 7 6 5 4 3

WEBPAGE

Author biographical note:

Mildred Thompson Barnum was born in Long Beach, California and raised in Grinnell, Iowa. There she intended to remain but destiny and her husband, Stanley, had other plans.

Following WW2, the family settled in Mountain View, Missouri, where she continues to reside. A widely differening career included personal, secretarial, and accounting services, insurance agent and broker, editor of the *Mountain View Standard,* artist and writer. *The Stake Is Gold* is her first novel.

Today, she enjoys visiting family and friends, a game of bridge, cruising the library, practicing and playing the organ in the Presbyterian Church, and occasional trips to Branson, Missouri to see the shows or to Springfield to shop.

Gratitude expression: DeAnne Mulder, cover illustrator:

My sincere thanks go to DeAnne Mulder whose drawings are featured in children's coloring books all over the Ozarks. Not only did she provide the perfect drawing for this book cover but also she helped put enough starch in my ego to submit this manuscript for publishing.

Gratitude expression: Donnie Russell/ Steve Williams

My eternal gratitude goes also to Donnie Russell and Steve Williams who have kept me from impatiently demolishing my demon computer and all my papers. Thanks, guys!

Category:
        Fiction

Grade Level:
        Adult
Website keywords
        Barnum
        Jinx
Stake
        Gold
        Doc
        Kale
        Rocky
        Ozark Mountains
        Red Rock
        Murder
        Poker

Brief book description:

In spite of the inquest findings, Doc and Rocky were certain that Cran was murdered --- but was it necessary that they lose other friends also? And could Gerty forgive?

Full book description:

Every time old Doc threaded his beat up cab-over pickup up tight around the fender high brush and pulled up at the path to Red Rock, he was reminded of Cran's death and its aftermath.

In the old days, there were Rocky, and Kale and Jake and E.L. and John and the rest of the guys - - - and the wife, and Gerty and Canody - - - all gone separate ways. Yet they were still in his heart.

He recalled the day when Gerty called a halt, other troubling things like murder were happening, and both Doc and Rocky had rushed to another violent scene.

But it wasn't all worry. There were the poker nights, those nights when the seven guys pulled up to that big, round table and the chips began to rattle.

"I lost some friends – but I gained some, too. Rocky, for one," Doc thought. " He and his sons will soon be here - - - "

For some minutes the old man stood breathing into his being the quiet and serenity of the area then he turned and trudged up the rise toward Red Rock.

JINX BARNUM

The Stake Is Gold

PROLOGUE

October, 2006

DOC:

The old man threaded the beat up cab-over pickup through fender high brush, over stumps and rocks, up tight around the foot of the bluff and over the room sized slab of red rock, cut the motor and sat starring into the golden sunset. He was tired yet he was excited as he was excited every autumn during the deer-hunting season.

v

Trees were silhouetted against the blazing sky: oaks with withered leaves shivering in the breeze, bared walnut boles with crooked limbs stretched, white barked sycamore guarding the watercress at their feet, pine forming a saw-toothed background to the scene.

The river at this place looked quiet and peaceful reflecting in muted hues of yellow, pink, green, lavender the brilliance of the setting sun yet the water moved swiftly, its current carrying fallen leaves and twigs toward the riffles ahead. As Doc watched the colors faded, the water darkening, the riffles shining among the rocks.

On his left and across the river the bluff rose towering over the scrabble at its foot. Blue Bluff it was called, one of the highest and most spectacular in the Ozark Mountains. Its shadow swiftly covered the scene below as the sun dipped below the horizon.

"I need to get a move on," old Doc thought. "Rocky and the boys will be here soon," but he continued to sit letting the peace and quiet soothe his tired soul. This was God's rock garden as Cran used to say, the place where Doc always hid when he'd had enough of life's problems. Funny how being in this one place always brought Cran to mind.

Rocky and the boys were coming. Maybe later after camp was set up, after the fried fish and potatoes were eaten they would sit around the fire and talk about the old days. Doc needed that; maybe it would be good for Rocky, too.

"I wonder if the boys have ever heard about Cran?" he thought. "I wonder if Rocky has ever told them about those days when he was courting Gretchen and searching for murderers?"

Perhaps not. The boys, Bill and Chuck, hadn't had the Ozark upbringing their father had known but they'd had nearly everything else. When they were still tykes Rocky won a State Representative seat so he and Gretchen had moved the family to Jefferson City and from there they'd gone on to D.C. where he'd served in the Senate these past fifteen years.

"The boys aren't lacking education but they've never known the peace and quiet of this place," Doc thought. "But now --?

He climbed stiffly out of the old vehicle, his arthritic knees and hips slowing him, and began setting up his camp with patience and determination. They would be here soon.

ROCKY:

> Well, it's one for the money,
> Two for the show,
> Three to get ready and go, cats, go
> but don't –
> Don't you step on my blue suede
> shoes.
> You can do anything but
> Stay off my blue suede shoes ---

It was difficult to tell who sang the loudest, Elvis on the Golden Oldies radio broadcast or Rocky sitting behind the wheel of his rattling old electioneering van. Rocky was back in Missouri, back in the Ozarks, back to his beginnings driving the deep purple truck with the bright yellow legend "**VOTE FOR ROCKY POTTS**" that had helped him reach for his dream. He couldn't have been happier.

As a child Rocky had 'learned to swim in this

river, explore the sandstone caves, fish the streams, hunt for deer. He'd hiked the lanes, floated the rivers, learned the characteristics of such places as "Fishnet Cove", "Lone Pine Creek" and "Egghead Spring", laughed and cried with the people and finally become a local icon of honesty and service to the district. He'd traveled a long way through the years but sometimes, like today, he was glad to be home.

The ancient van grated over the rock-strewn trail, its brakes squealing at the sudden down hill plunge then groaning to a stop at the river's edge.

"Hey, Doc," he shouted.

"Ho!"

"Where are you?"

"None of your business," Doc laughed. "Go

on up to Red Rock. I'm setting up camp there."

Red Rock. The room sized slab of iron-ore-studded rock marking the entrance to Blue Cave. An excellent place to camp, Rocky recalled, sheltered from the wind by the bluff behind it and elevated enough to protect from flash floods.

Leaving the van, Rocky headed up the steep pass pushing through the forest overgrowth then up the rocky grade, his boots swishing through the dry, wild grasses. There were turkey tracks, deer tracks. A covey of quail startled him with sudden flight.

God! How good it was to be back in these peaceful hills, to flee from the noise and frantic pace of D.C. The colors, the scent, the whispering of the breeze through the trees, the

soft rustling of dried grass -"Balm to my soul,"
Rocky thought.

Doc pushed through the trees. "Think the
boys will be able to find this place?" he asked
as he threw down an armful of wood.

"I hope so. I sent Chuck a map of the area;
furthermore, I've described the place to them
so often that they can probably recite my
directions word for word. If they can find their
way around Europe, surely they will be able to
locate our area of the Ozarks. Yes, they'll be
here, Doc. Count on it!"

THE "BOYS':

They were in the Explorer, loaded down with
camping gear, hunting equipment, food and

beer.

"Do you know where you're going?" Chuck asked.

"I hope so," Bill answered. "If you had remembered to bring your map, we would be considerably more certain, wouldn't we?"

"Shit! If I'd stopped to find that map before I left the office, I'd be there yet."

Bill hunched over the steering wheel, his eyes on the road, his muscles tense, his mood sharp but at Chuck's response he was sorry for his bitter words. There was no way that he would put up with the frantic day-to-day demands that Chuck had to tackle. Representative George P. Dade of Pennsylvania was, Bill knew, something of a loose cannon in the House and Chuck as his assistant had to cover the old man's tracks.

Couldn't ask for a more difficult job than that; however, the job could be a first rate stepping stone toward a seat in the House for Chuck.

"Chuck has money, he has women and he has notoriety," Bill thought. "If that's what he wants, more power to him. But I wonder if he's happy? He's close to thirty years old. Doesn't he ever think about settling down with a wife, a family, a home of his own?"

To Bill, these were the things that counted. "I don't know what I would do without Jenny and Crissy; they make my life whole," Bill realized again. "Too often I'm held up at the office but Jenny doesn't grouse around at my long working hours and my precious little Crissy - - - Darn! What did I ever do without a daughter to love?"

Still, he knew he'd needed to get away,

needed these few days to unwind. "You know, Chuck," he said, "this trip is probably good for both of us. Give us some time out, space to relax and enjoy. I'm looking forward to it."

"Yes, so am I," Chuck answered, "and Dad, I think, needs it even more. He's more stressed than either of us." He paused, and then continued, "I can see why he's drawn to these hills. Even at this time of year, they are impressive. - - There's the red rag on that tree. We turn here, don't we?"

The trail was no problem for the Explorer; however Bill wasn't used to having to drive carefully to dodge stumps, boulders and tree limbs. Downshifting, he forded the creek, climbed again then groaned down the grade and around the foot of the bluff to pull up beside Doc's pickup.

"Good! You made it," Rocky grinned, grabbing each son in a hefty bear hug.

"We heard you coming," Doc added. "Bring your gear on up to the camp. Supper is cooking. Hope you're hungry."

Doc watched as the three men loaded themselves down with the gear then labored toward the camp.

Yes! He grinned. Those boys were just what he'd expected, both tall men and muscular like Rocky, handsome, blond and blue eyed like Gretchen, Chuck the budding politician, Bill the CPA.

"Rocky can certainly be proud," he thought, "- and they should be proud of their Pa."

In fact, he intended to see to it.

CHAPTER ONE

February, 1966

Doc:

You couldn't expect a fifty-year-old buzzard like me to set the world on fire. All I wanted to do was save enough for some retirement income - you know, money salted away to bring in enough interest so the wife and I could eat regularly, keep a roof over our heads, maybe take a little jaunt now and then to see the country, no spectacular riches, no big-assed "keeping up with the Jones"', just comfort and peace and reprieve from the everlasting complaining I heard in my office day in and day out.

That's the reason I liked Crannahan so well: he didn't complain. He'd bellyache like hell about a drop in the stock market or about the rats in his roof or the river flooding his cellar but I swear I never once heard him whine about his 'condition'. He'd never become acquainted with self-pity, I guess, so he was one of the few who could walk into the office and say, "Doc, I've got a pain," without shedding tears all over the place. He could have laughed and joked if he'd been bit by a rattlesnake - after, of course, killing the varmint and cussing the air blue for an hour. That's the way he was. His complaints were entertaining, you might say, so I enjoyed talking to him.

But he had his faults. For one thing, he was a rough talker. He'd come into the office, slouch down in a chair in the reception room, light up a choking cigar and proceed to flatter all the old girls sitting there by telling some outrageous tale having to do with sex. Picture him in the middle of a room full of females, him grinning from ear to ear and them needing doses of tranquilizer to settle them down. You know, underneath, you have to admire a man like that, as brash as hell but getting away with it and gaining secret admirers in the process.

He looked like the biggest hayseed in the Ozarks most of the time. He'd been a mighty handsome man in his youth but drink and fast living had taken their toll and only the tail end of his good looks was apparent when I first met him. It must have been pure wear and tear that made his bushy head of hair and stiff mustache that iron gray color and probably as a result of the booze he drank ("to

keep my liver washed out," he used to say),
the blue of his eyes had become sort of watery
and yellow around the edges. His cheeks held
a peculiar red tinge - a holdover from frost bite
in the early days - but he'd retained that
beautiful classic Roman profile that makes
female hearts beat faster and he stood tall and
straight and proud. People had a habit of
turning to look at him twice.

He dressed like a bum, always wearing an
old pair of khaki britches - usually decorated
with paint stains, a plaid flannel shirt with an
elbow out and a couple of buttons missing,
and a straw hat, once white, grown old and
decrepit with the man and he didn't give a
damn. For some reason, the worse he looked
the more magnetism he seemed to have.

But I don't choose a friend for his looks. If he

can carry on an intelligent conversation, if he can laugh and if he pays his bills, I'm very likely to like him whether his presence decorates my office or not. What are a few cigar ashes or mud or manure between friends?

Actually, the only thing that Cranahan and I had in common (except, maybe, a slight tinge of slovenliness) was a mutual interest in the stock market. Every time I got a few bucks, I liked to buy a share or two of something and as I invested in more diverse companies, I developed what my wife called a market mania. I kept charts of the ups and downs and the do's and the don'ts and I was always looking for a new book on the subject or for a new friend who was interested likewise. That's where Cran fit in - he lived, breathed stock market and had a very successful record. Probably as a consequence of the authority I gave to his words on the subject, he enjoyed draping himself over a chair in my office spouting information.

The seed of his investments had been inherited by his wife, that's true, but in short order he'd made a hundred grand grow into several millions and I admired his success. He not only knew which companies had changed policy or kicked out a dead beating director or diversified or did a little kooky maneuvering to cut down on the tax bite or won a court battle, he could also tell which director was shacking up with which company bigwig's wife, what secretary had recently absconded to some God-forsaken place with an unhealthy amount of the profits, - in short, where the action was, licit and illicit. All this was like honey dripping into the beehive of my dreams of success and wealth; consequently, I was probably his number one audience.

I remember one day Cran was sitting with one leg draped over the arm of the chair in my back office puffing up a steam on his thin, black stogie and shouting at me and all asunder about his many investments and, as usual, he began to get riled when he got off on the subject of real estate. Later when I looked back on the conversation, I recalled just one little hint that came in handy. "Like that damn farm out there," he shouted. "A thousand acres of rocks and scrub brush, whicker grass and jack oak, black-berry briers and snakes, and rats, and 'coon, and the only good thing on it is the river and even that goes on a rampage every time the heavens spill down a little sprinkle and then the cellar fills up and the damn rats have to go swimming for a while. Why I bought the place, I don't rightly know. When you own property, you always have to look after it."

"Just the other day I thought I saw smoke coming from the chimney of the old house on the West quarter so one of these days I'm going to have to climb that damn mountain to see if there's a squatter there. He couldn't hurt anything short of setting the woods on fire but I'll have to check, nevertheless."

"Now if that money was in General Motors I wouldn't be half so bothered. Someone else could look after it and just send me my share of the gleanings. Why the hell would anyone want to unload a bunch of loot on a pile of

God's forgotten rock garden like I did on that farm?"

Actually the farm is a beautiful place. The hills are doubled up against the little river which tumbles down through the middle like a ribbon of silver and the thick covering of trees, pine and oak and walnut, filter the sunlight and keep the ground cool and moist. There are bluffs and rapid, tumbling waters and deep, mysterious pools and cool caves and beautifully noisy birds and wild animals and – well, I think he was right to call it "God's rock garden."

There used to be three houses on the place. Just at the entrance to the property on the main road, there stood a little cottage, usually empty and canting northwards. At one time it was a pretty little place all surrounded as it was with blossoming peach and pear trees but the sands of time left its mark and one day a puff of wind blew it into a pile of rubble.

Just up the river a way there is an ancient two-story house built of hard oak timbers which has withstood the battering winds and rains for a hundred years. It stands on a high, naked hill – one of the highest hereabouts – with the winter wind whipping around it and the summer sun beating down upon it alone and lonely. No one knows just what was in the builder's mind, whether he placed the structure by design or accident, but, whichever, it stands in such a line that as the winter sun sets its orange rays are caught and reflected and concentrated like so many fires from hell through the windows. Gives one an eerie feeling just looking at it.

Then there is the house that Cran built. It has gone to seed now but at that time it was a beauty. He chose a spot at the edge of the valley on a rocky promontory around which the river rustles and sings and designed it to blend into its setting like a ruby into a mountain of gold. It was long and low, warm looking, welcoming. And it was built with love, I think, for the family who left and seldom returned.

That house was Cran's one great effort as an architect. He'd had a superior education with a degree in architectural engineering (or whatever it's called) but along about the time he was starting to enter the rat race to fame and fortune, someone introduced him to Melody.

"Now there was my chance," he told me.

11

"She was young and beautiful, her Pa was rolling in dough and she was in heat. And who quarrels with conditions like that? She got knocked up the first month after she came home from finishing school - which turned out to be a good deal because if she hadn't, her Pa would have shipped her off to Europe or somewhere. He very nearly did anyway but one night the maid found her passed out in the bathtub with both wrists slashed and the old man discovered that he couldn't stand the sight of blood - especially hers."

Things were hectic for them at first. Cran balked at going to work in the family chemical plant (and probably the old man balked at asking him to) so he and Melody high-tailed it to New York. Before their daughter was born he'd tried three jobs and been canned from all of them either for appearing on the job all liquored up or for cussing out the boss. He'd gone to Atlantic City to look for work when Melody had the baby so she'd walked to the free clinic - luckily no more than three blocks away - and was delivered fast and easy. From that time on things were in and out for them, I guess, rich when he was working, poor, lonely and blue when the jobs folded but relatively sober and immensely happy with one another, nonetheless.

Fortunately - or unfortunately depending on how you look at it - Melody's Pa didn't live too long after the birth of their second child and after the funeral her Ma came east, picked up the whole brood, bag and baggage, and took them back to Chicago with her. I gathered that Cran was expected to be-a kind of glorified messenger boy around there, hopping and jumping to his mother-in-law's whims, and he began to build a strong hatred and resentment. It wasn't long, then, until he was taking his anger out on Melody so she took to the bottle to brighten up her day. Anyway, they babysat the old lady until she died then waited around for the glad news of the will.

Except that it wasn't as glad as they had hoped. It seems that Pa hadn't felt exactly generous toward Cran and he probably figured that leaving money where Cran could put his hands on it was like putting it down the drain so he willed Melody only the hundred thou. Melody, no doubt in her cups at the time, signed it over to Cran and he, to everyone's surprise, turned out to be a mighty good man at the till.

They were glad to leave Chicago and move with their kids to live a life of freedom in their house on the river - freedom from the strictures of society and freedom from want - and after the children left, loneliness. And the lonelier it got, the more pathetic Melody got and the more she drank and finally she climbed into her Cadillac and drove it over the bridge and into the river and there she lay, beautiful, fragile, a lady to the core, drunk and dead.

So that's how it was with Cran.

CHAPTER TWO

DOC:

Cran was a heavy drinker, too, but not too heavy. He always had a case of hooch in the house and a fifth in his pickup, it's true, but he wasn't a drunk. Just to be on the safe side I would check his vitals now and then and considering his age and the abuse he gave his body, he was in pretty good shape. That's one of the reasons why I was so surprised when he died.

It was on a Thursday along about noon when I answered the jangling office phone and recognized his daughter's honeyed tones dripping from the wire. "Dr. Farlin," she oozed, "I've been trying to call Dad and I can't get an answer. I've tried for nearly a week. Can you tell me where to find him?"

Well now! Trying to look back through the hair-tearing week I'd been having through the flu season, I couldn't rightly remember when I'd last seen him. Was it Monday? Or Tuesday? Or last Saturday? Or two weeks ago Saturday? You know how it is: with so many things loading on your mind it's hard to pin down a specific time or date so I hemmed and hawed and tried to think but the false honeyed voice on the other end of the line was distracting - was irritating me - and all I could think of was that I don't trust people who talk like that. It's not honest. Anyway, I finally had to admit that I didn't know where Cran was and then I had to promise to look him up and tell him that his ritzy daughter was calling and why couldn't he stay at home and answer his phone instead of expecting me to take out to find him?

It was evening before I had a chance to start hunting. The wife and I drove the eleven miles to his house, knocked, and when no one answered, walked in – he never did lock his doors. "Any one who'd come 'way out there is a fool and needs some place to hide," I've heard him say – well, we walked in, hollered, looked in all the rooms and then behind the doors, under the beds, in the closets, in the cellar and the barn (the horse had a reproachful expression on his kisser and his stall was empty of feed) and over the hill and every place we could think of. No answer. The house was cold and the wife wondered why the windows were open and the thermostat had been turned down. Since our last warm day was several days past, I began to wonder too.   .

It wasn't only the open windows and the chill of the house that puzzled me. There were other things like the open bottle of booze, half full, that stood on the table beside a plate smeared with dried up, leftover food and the newspaper lying open beside it. The date? – this struck me right between the eyes! - February 18th. Four days ago! Where was today's paper? Cran couldn't live without his daily paper. What had happened?

We finally gave up, the wife and I, and went home to roost but that newspaper kept bothering me. I guess I tossed around some because after a spell the wife rose right up in bed (pulling off my side of the covers, naturally) and told me, for goodness' sake, to quit worrying about that bum and go to sleep. He was of age, she pointed out, and perfectly capable of taking care of himself. Not my responsibility, she said. And then she cuddled down with her head on the soft place in my shoulder and she kissed the back of my ear and she threw her leg over mine and I forgot all about Cran – in fact, after a while, I went right off to sleep like I always do after an evening of fun and games.

Next day, though, we were both worrying again. Morning passed and he didn't show; afternoon, we kept expecting him to pop in; by evening, we decided that we'd better search some more. It seemed mighty peculiar that he'd go off and leave his house in a mess and the windows wide open this time of year.

For February, the day was fair to middling.

20

The late afternoon sun was still shining and though there was a chill in the air, the grass was beginning to green up and the wife pointed out a couple of jonquils bobbing on the south side of a hill. Since there was no leaves on the trees this early in the season, we could see some distance and we never get our fill of the beauty of the Ozarks.

Well, we were bowling along, enjoying the scenery, when just as we topped a hill, off to the West I saw the hulk of Cran's old two-story house. There it stood, stark naked along the horizon, and right about then I remembered him wrapping himself over my chair and saying, "I'll have to see if there's a squatter there."

You've heard people say that the hairs will rise on the back of the neck? They do. Mine did.

We had a hell of a time finding the road that led to the old house. It was all overgrown with weeds and brush and thistles and if we hadn't seen the marker near, we never would have found it. Apparently others had had some trouble likewise because someone had marked the turn by tying a piece of red cloth to an oak branch nearby. After driving through about a quarter mile of dense and tangled brush, we angled down into the narrow, little valley that slopes across the land to the river and along there, the going was easy but it got bad again when we began to climb back into the hills and when we finally dropped down to Hunter's Creek, right close to where it joins the river, we had to admit to ourselves that our Buick just wasn't made for that kind of going. We could see the tracks that Cran's pickup had made fording the creek but it was one of those high-axle jobs made especially for this land. Ours just would not do it and live to tell the tale.

There is always water in the creek in the early spring though ordinarily it goes dry later and now was no exception but it looked to us as though, since we were feeling young and agile, we might be able to jump from one stone to the next and with luck we could get across without getting wet. Naturally, lady luck wasn't playing any favorites. Just because it was early spring and the sun was shining didn't give us the right as old and decrepit as we were to feel young and gay and adventurous without paying for it.

Did you ever climb an Ozark hill? With your shoes sloshing full of water? You'd swear that it grows taller and longer and higher... The brambles cling to your clothes, you can break your neck – er, an ankle – if you step in a hole, your lungs begin to ache and breathing becomes the first and foremost problem. Maybe I was just out of condition; maybe I should have taken up hill climbing as a hobby – and then, again, maybe exercise like that should be left for younger folks.

Sure enough, there stood Cran's pickup at the side of the house. Up close, the house looked enormous with its sun baked timber siding, windowless windows, and broken steps – Edger Allen Poe would have loved the place but I had the feeling it wasn't exactly my cup of tea. The wife felt the same, I guess, because when I tried to get her to stay outside she took one wild look around at the animal tracks in the mud at her feet, grabbed my hand and held on for dear life. So in we went together, timorous and hesitant you might say, through the sagging back door and there he lay face down on the floor with an empty hooch bottle in one hand and a pill box in the other dead as a door nail.

The smell in the room was something fierce, the stink of dead and rotting flesh plus some sweetish odor that I couldn't pin down. Naturally, a doctor's inclination when he comes across a corpse is to look over the remains to find the cause so I turned him over, lifted an eyelid, looked into a staring, dead, blue eye, looked around for cuts or bumps or bruises or bullet holes or something – anything- but all I could find was that damned empty bottle and a little white box labeled Phenobarbital. Now who in hell had given him that, I wondered. Not me! He'd never needed it – or, that is, he'd never mentioned any such need to me. And what the devil was that smell?

Just as I'd known she'd do, my wife was having a full-sized fit. When I touched Cran, she screamed; when I opened his eye, she tried to look over my shoulder – while she screamed; when we left the place, she was still screaming; when I slapped her, she stopped the noise and gave me a dirty look. She's a tough old bird and has seen a few stiffs in her time but none quite as ripe as this one. It got the best of her for a while. What the hell! Even I felt green and sick!

Yes, I know. I should have reported to the police immediately upon finding the body –

but I didn't. At that moment, it seemed to me that the wife was more important. I needed to get her calmed down in her own little nest Then and only then would I tackle the Sheriff. Therefore, there being nothing more we could do for Cran, we left him to stumble down the hill and across the creek to our car.

"Look!" the wife shouted. She had turned around to look at the old house once more and, sure enough, there was the orange light of the setting sun shining with a magnified brilliance, sparkling through the windows as though the fires of Satan himself raged within. And who are we to know His pleasure? The hairs stood stiff on the back of my neck again.

CHAPTER THREE

DOC:

Doc Crafton, the coroner in our county in those days, was a dumb ass. You know the kind. One of those smart-alecks who spouts great technical terms, puffs himself up as though he has the wisdom of Christ and hasn't actually the wit to come in out of the rain. The only reason he was coroner was that his big words didn't cure the illnesses of his patients so they didn't stay with him – they cluttered up the offices of the rest of us – and his income dropped 'way below his estimation of himself. So he took the job for the money, for the title, and for the notoriety, I suppose, and the county put up with his ineptness simply because no one else would have the job. The rest of us had too much to do already.

Figuring that I would have a better chance of tagging along to watch the police investigation by being on the spot to insist, I had decided to report Cran's death by sailing down to the local police office rather than grabbing the phone to make the call. Kale Riley, the city marshal, was there (for a change) and was downright interested in what I had to say.

"Yeah, I know the old place," he said. "There is where old Moziah Robinson had his still 'till the state revenuers found it and hustled him off to the pen. I remember, during prohibition, when Pa'd hunt up old Moze on the street of a Saturday, slip him a buck and later on Pa'd find a convenient bottle of white lightening under that old tree with the red rag tied to it. In those days, that weren't the way up to the

29

house. They was another way to come in from the other side. That tree with the rag was on the back of the property. The other road's been blocked off years ago – when they made the three-mile cut for the new highway – and as far as I know, no one's been able to use it since."

Well all this was interesting to me and I liked Kale but I kept having the feeling that Cran was mighty uncomfortable up there in all that smell and that someone should be giving him some decent treatment for a change so I lost my temper – which is easy for me, now and again – and suggested that he get a move on and get someone out there to do something.

Kale's drawl is so slow that I get impatient just waiting for him to get the words out of his mouth. "Yeah. Well, I'll call the sheriff and I suppose he'll have to get hold of Doc Crafton. There's not much hope of doing this without letting Crafton in on it. He'd holler all the way to Washington."

No use dragging out this story. Suffice it to say that we finally got started, Crafton, Rocky, Kale and me.

Crafton was all of six four and must have weighed in at around two hundred forty and the cowboy hat he wore made him look about a foot taller. He'd stand with his head 'way up there in the clouds looking down on us little folk with a superior smirk on his puss as though he was the loving Father with sympathy but command over all us poor mortals. His little, dainty, pretty white hands with the manicured nails and the fancy, flashing, fake diamonds looked downright incongruous, especially when he carried his officious looking little bag – and he carried it as tenderly as I would if it was loaded with hooch.

Your Dad – the sheriff – he was a different proposition. First place, his pa, T.R. Potts, felt poetic when his first son was born and named him Rocky – Rocky Amoricious Potts – so the boy grew up to be quite a scrapper just trying to live up to his name. As you know, he won't take crap from anyone, ever. He's not very big – about the size of most hillbillies – long, lean and leathery he is and tough as cow hide – but he's a good square Joe with a fair-mindedness that makes him a natural for his job. I always figured that the county was lucky to have him and I certainly want him on my side if the going gets tough. But he's about as stubborn as Doc Crafton – not quite, but almost.

So after a bunch of hemming and hawing and conferring, the four of us headed out to rescue Cran from the jam he was in. Rocky, Doc, Kale (who, as city marshal, had no authority whatsoever outside the city limits but who wouldn't miss this little excursion for anything) and me. Of course we all knew that I didn't have any business out there either but by then I'd begun to realize that in all the first fuss and hurry with my wife screaming and my nerve shredding under the impact of that smell, I hadn't taken time to look around. Questions were beginning to plague me and perhaps Rocky hoped that I might spot something – something that I'd missed earlier – that would provide a clue or two.

Things were just like they were when the wife and I had been there and the smell was still present, clear and sickening. We had to breathe through our handkerchiefs – doc used a disposable Kleenex – in order to stay in the house. This time, though, I just stood back and watched the proceedings.

The room – kitchen, it was – was clean! This hit me all of a sudden. Why, if the house had been empty for years, wasn't it covered with dust? I don't mean clean as it would have been with a good woman keeping house but clean, instead, as though someone had shifted the dust around and pushed some of it out the door with the broom. The old coal oil stove had stuff burned on the top – like grease and such – layers of it firmly baked on until it would have been impossible to clean but it had coal oil in it, I lit it and it worked. Rocky told me to leave things alone and stop tampering with the evidence but I ignored him. Before long, I saw him back up to the fire like a purring tabby – until the coal oil smell began to mix with the general stink of the place.

Close to the stove stood an ancient cupboard with a chipped enamel top and inside there were one or two old plates, cups, pans and stuff. Hanging over the cabinet – mixing spoons, flour sifter, rolling pin – things that most housewives like to keep handy – yes, clean there, too. In the middle of the room there was an old, square, oak table (the heavy kind that takes four men and a boy to heft) and three broken chairs. Beyond that, against the far wall, was a couch with a lumpy cotton mattress and a bunch of ragged and scattered bedding on it. Other than this, the room was empty. As I've already said, there weren't any curtains at the windows and there was no covering on the floor – just wide, pine flooring with dust seeping through from underneath. Little feathers of straw lay in the corners and a few cartons of Pepsi and Sprite huddled under one window. I noticed, too, that there were panes in the windows and I had thought that all the windows had been busted out long ago.

The rest of the house, when I went through it, was empty except for a few broken pieces of furniture and – yep! I'd been right! – there was shattered window glass beneath the gaping windows. The main thing, though, was that the second story held a decade of dust and cobwebs whereas those two back rooms of the first floor (the kitchen and what once upon a time must have been a dining room) had no cobwebs and only about an eighth as much dust – which wasn't enough.

To Crafton, the evidence was held in Cran's two hands: the bottle and the pillbox with the word PHENOBARBITAL typed on it.

"M, hum", he um, humped. "A clear case of accidental suicide. Alcoholic barbiturate poisoning. Party of the first part lying on the bed, drinking, trying to sleep. Alcohol effect of relaxant negated by habitual drinking; therefore, party used x number of Phenobarbital pills to induce sleep. Poisoning resulted. Party moved off of the bed but fell to the floor." He actually talked that way.

Bed? Hell! Cran wouldn't lie on those rags on that old sofa - yet it did look like the logical explanation. If I hadn't known Cran better I might have jumped to the some conclusion. But this time things looked awry to me – too circumstantial. And there were other things - - - "You will be making a lab test?" I asked.

He glared at me with all the dignified hurt of an insulted billy goat. "Sir?"

I'd have laughed if I hadn't been so disgusted.

"My dear doctor," he continued. "If you would deign to peruse a text you would find that alcohol and barbiturates have a chemical reaction which may very well result in the death of the patient when taken to excess. Mr. Crannahan was well known in the use of alcoholic beverages and it is quite simple these days to purchase Phenol for use when needed. One need only complain to the local druggists of the inability to sleep and thereby procure the illicit drug. I have always maintained that local pharmacists are most careless in their dispensation of drugs without proper authority."

He should have heard what the local druggists thought of him!

"I know what the book says," I thundered back, "but that doesn't prove a thing! Cran didn't need sleeping pills. He was healthy as an ox and was always bragging about being able to drop off for a catnap any time he felt like it. Besides, I think you should look around this house a little. Someone has been here. Who the hell do you suppose put coal oil in that stove? Cran didn't. You can bet your doggies on that. He wasn't about to keep this place supplied with oil and cooking utensils and all that crap. He was too fond of his creature comforts. No, sir! Look around."

He wasn't the kind to take a suggestion gracefully. Turning away from me, he shrugged. "That's not my department."

Well, now, I'm not afraid of a fight – I'll get right in there with anyone who is willing to take me on but there is no use fighting a fool so I pulled up a mite. Maybe Rocky would listen. I turned questioningly to him but he simply shrugged and would have none of it.

So, O.K. That was it, for now. Crafton had all the authority in this matter; I had none. I shrugged, looked questioningly again at Rocky then turned to go.

"Just a minute, my good man." Crafton grabbed my arm, holding me while he spoke through his disposable Kleenex. "You three will have to move the cadaver." He coughed and I noticed happily that his color had changed a bit. "The gurney is in the back of the wagon." He cut for the door. I guess his Kleenex had a hole in it. Ha!

Crafton had taken possession of the wagon about half an hour after his votes were counted on Election Day and he drove the battered old machine as though it were a badge of authority. It was an old Ford bought by the County second hand from the city of St. Louis, equipped with a narrow front seat, two jump seats, and the gurney. And there were additions – all kinds of well-kept, shiny, emergency equipment. Damned if the idiot didn't even have scalpels in there.

Nervousness and reaction and then the sight of that fancy, shining, operating room all set up in the back end of that old crate must have been too much for me. I laughed. I laughed until I was rolling in the grass. I laughed until my stomach hurt. I laughed with tears in my eyes. I laughed until Kale and Rocky picked me up, dusted me off, slapped me on the back, cussed me out and left me with the haughty ass-hole to sober up while they handled the messy remains between them, wrapping it in a sterile sheet, laying it on the gurney, loading the gurney into the back of the wagon in the midst of all that beautiful chrome, rolling down all the windows to let the chill of the night blow away the smell – which was impossible – then climbing into the jump seats leaving the idiot to drive his rolling office out of the brush and me to hunch morosely beside him, shivering now and then from cold, from fatigue or from pure horror, I don't know which. Silently we drove back to town, each with his own thoughts to keep him company.

Crafton was in a hurry to get rid of me apparently so he stopped to let me off at my house. And then – well, maybe he's a decent sort after all.

He said quietly, "Good night, Doc. Don't you worry. I'll take care of things. And, Doc, my sympathy. You must have loved the bastard."

Rocky:

Look at him! Old Doc. There he sits, this old man in his boots, mackinaw and corduroy pants, hunkered down before the campfire, reminiscing as though Cran's death happened yesterday. More than thirty years ago it happened - -

Before Cranahan died I didn't know Doc very well. He must have been somewhere around fifty years old at that time and the years were beginning to show. Not too tall - close to six feet, I suppose - with the beginning of a paunch, a ruddy complexion, shockingly blue eyes with laugh wrinkles at the corners, a white halo around his bald pate.

And a great personality. Everybody liked him. He's honest and outspoken but not brutally so; he's sympathetic with his patients (or anyone else with a sob story); he's intelligent, tactful, patient, poised, self-confident - a hell of a man. But stubborn and tenacious as a pit bull if he sees a wrong that needs to be righted.

I'll never forget his actions the day he found Cran. I had pulled up in front of the police station in answer to Kale's call and Doc came tearing out of the building, grabbed hold of the door of my patrol car and had it opened before I could stop. "Where's the coroner?* he was shouting.

Hell. I didn't know. Kale nodded at my unspoken question so I answered as reasonably as I could. "He's on his way."

Doc turned his back, jammed his hands in his pockets, and began pacing around the parking lot, mumbling to himself, turning every few minutes to give me a dirty look.

When the Coroner pulled in, Doc jumped up and planted his backside in the front seat of the van with a frowned I-dare-you expression on his face. Today, of course, investigators wouldn't put up with such nonsense; they would secure the property absolutely refusing to let him return to the site of the suspicious death and protecting it from trespass from any other interested parties no matter how involved they might be. But in this case we simply accepted the inevitable. We'd have had to hog-tie Doc to keep him from tagging along.

Besides if the truth were known I had more faith in Doc's judgment than in Crafton's. Experience had led me to believe that the man had some kind of sixth sense about unexpected occurrences.

"I just can't believe it!" Doc was saying as we made our way toward Cranahan's property. "Cran mentioned not long ago that he needed to check this old house because he suspected that someone had holed up there but he certainly didn't act too excited about it. Someone was there - that's obvious - and

Cran would have accepted a drink - that's typical - but the Phenol! That's the kicker. Why would he have taken Phenobarbital?"

I'd grown up in these Ozarks but I'd certainly never been in the area where Doc directed us. After fording the creek we followed an old, narrow path - looked like a wagon path - overgrown with weeds and thistles. The road wound through a thick stand of post oak and pine towering over a thick tangle of underbrush and not until we finally reached the once-cleared area could we see the house. Slowly, we piled out of the van and stared at it. From where we stood, it looked enormous. Fragments of yellow paint were peeling off the hardwood siding. A front porch extending the length of the house sagged toward the three weather-bent front steps. The scarred front door boasted an antique etched glass and a brass knocker, now green. Long, narrow, evenly spaced windows stared out at a small, overgrown lawn. Like Doc said, it stands high on a steep hill and I could see that one would be able to see the upper story of the house from a distance.

In the past two decades great improvements in technological advances toward solving crimes have been made; unfortunately, in the 1950's and early `60's in the rural areas of the Ozarks, we were expected to solve crimes by the seat of our pants - - - but I'm getting ahead of the story. This was not, so far, a crime scene. It truly appeared to be an accidental death with some very interesting side effects.

For one thing, the sweet odor that Doc was

harping about but could not recognize was the scent of marijuana and many of the regular household gadgets at the scene were the kinds of utensils that pot growers used to harvest the crop. For another, it seemed obvious that someone had been spending a lot of time in the house but had had the time and the sense to clear out before Doc's arrival on the scene.

It was typical of Doc to light the fire in the stove because, number one, he suspected that someone had been spending a considerable amount of time in the house and would have needed heat during the past winter and, number two, he wanted to aggravate Crafton.

And Crafton was indeed aggravated. His examination of the corpse had been sketchy to say the least; however, there was no way that the body could be moved until Kale and I had taken photos, made notes and done all the other preliminary things that we needed to do while Crafton was covering his nose with one hand and trying to hurry the proceedings with the other. I was not the least bit surprised to hear his crack judgment as to the cause of Cran's death - nor was I surprised when Doc called him on it.

As Doc said, there was not much to see on the second story. Yes, some of the window panes were gone (most of the smashed glass lay in the refuse around the outside of the house), it was bare of furniture, the plumbing didn't work, faded wallpaper was peeling from the walls; in short, it appeared that whomever had been using the two first floor rooms had no intention of living permanently in the building.

I don't know what set Doc off when he began to laugh but I could certainly tell that it wasn't his normal he-haw. In fact it sounded more like hysteria. Kale and I were in the house packing the things that in our judgment were the most important bits of evidence but when we heard him, we lit for the door. We found him on one knee in the dust hanging onto the bumper of the van, gasping for breath with tears shining on his cheeks.

It didn't take long for Kale and me to decide that we needed to get the show on the road. We had taken care of the most important part of the investigation and it seemed unlikely that the house would be disturbed before morning so like Doc said, we loaded the corpse into the wagon, climbed in behind Crafton and Doc and headed for town. Any other investigation could wait until later.

But Doc- poor old boy. Thirty years and he's still rehashing the day. Will he ever get over the shock?

CHAPTER FOUR

Doc:

Cran's death didn't make too much of a stir in the community. He'd always been somewhat of an outlander respected because of his money and scorned because of his unorthodox way of life so - other than relishing the thought that "he got what he richly deserved" - there wasn't much comment and absolutely no ripple on the river of community life. A few attended the funeral out of curiosity to see how the family took it (the daughter came down from Chicago, tall, ugly, haughty, sarcastic, pretentious and domineering, and the son, effeminate and sickening, came up from New Orleans) and the only other public notices were those which appeared on the back page of the local gossip sheet: a simple eulogy giving the bare facts of his existence, and a disrespectful reference to his ungodly way of life in the printed sermon by the good Reverend Goodall. After a week the gossip died down and he was forgotten around town. His family - and his money - was gone and his remains were marked only by a huge pretentious gray stone which must have weighted down on his coffin something terrible.

The flue still raged and Gretchen Marti (my girl Friday), the wife and I were busy in the office, the wife in her lab and Gerty and I in the examination and treatment rooms. We were happy to drop the subject of Cran's death, to forget the horrible sight and smell of him, to erase from our minds the memory of his swimming blue eyes and raucous laugh and insolent manner. Now and then, late at night, I'd find myself worrying my suspicions as a dog gnaws at a bone picking at each bit of nudging evidence, something missed, something incomplete about the whole thing but mostly I let it alone. Life was too full of living problems.

It was perhaps three weeks later that the girl came in - a beautiful, slender, sad, worried girl. Gerty had taken the day off and the wife had slipped out of the lab to use the slack time to catch up on the books; that's the reason she was in the reception room when the girl entered. Well, the wife's ears popped up so to speak - you know, the way a wife automatically does when she senses sudden stiff competition to her love life - and from the other room I could tell that someone special had appeared because her voice got very chilly and proper and offhand. Usually, she sounds like a 727 coming in for a landing.

The girl answered her greeting in a low voice and at first I had to stretch to catch her words. Her voice reminded me of the low melody of a tenor sax, full of haunting, sexual overtones with a timbre of pure perfection.

"May I see the Doctor, please?"

"Surely. Your name?"

"Canody Pederson."

"And why did you wish to see him?" The wife can certainly be chilly when she wants to.

"Must I say, Ma'am? It's a personal matter."

I'd heard enough. Anyone who comes purring into my office with a voice like that can see me anytime!

The wife looked downright sour when I appeared but a good look at the girl was more than worth the chance I might be taking.

She was taller than most, slender - but not skinny, no! Definitely not skinny. Her body seemed to be all fluid movement, delicate but vital. Her face was indescribable in its beauty, with fine bones, wide-arched brown eyes, a soft and kissable mouth, a slightly olive complexion without a mar and soft brown hair, long, I guess, but now pulled back into a wide knot with a curl escaping at the nape of her neck. I felt an obscene desire to kiss the curl - a feeling I hadn't enjoyed for thirty-five years.

"I'm Dr. Farlin, young lady. Won't you come in?" I held the office door open for her and grinned when the wife marched in right behind her. "Now, what's the trouble?"

She stood in the center of the small room for all the world like a trapped squirrel looking from me to my wife to the window and back to me, trembling and twisting a white handkerchief in her hands. Her expression was a mixture of fright, pride and worry.

The wife stood there watching her for a moment then sympathy overtook the animosity in her expression and she tenderly touched her arm. "Come on, my dear. Won't you sit down? There now. That's better." Then, typically, she turned on me. "Doctor, why don't you lower that blind so the light won't shine in the poor girl's eyes?"

I could have guffawed. Just like the old lady, that, and now everything was back in perspective.

Canody's story sure surprised us. Who would have thought that Cran had had a girl friend - especially a beauty like this? He was always bragging about his virility and about all the different methods of making love he used but who believed him? He was nearly as old as I am and I haven't been able to carry on such antics for the past ten years. I was doing well to make it with the wife even.

As she listened, the wife got mad at Cran all over again as though if he hadn't already been done in she would be willing and able to do the job. I didn't see her reasoning. No sense blaming Cran for this girl's predicament. After all, she wasn't complaining. She had apparently enjoyed herself and would have liked things to continue as they were. Only now she had a problem.

"- - - so I think I'm pregnant."

Well! If she came here to ask me to undo that, she's out of luck!

"Don't misunderstand me," she hurried on, probably because she could read stubborn refusal written all over my face. "I want the baby. I'm going to name him Paul Cranahan and teach him all about his father and try to be a good mother to him. I loved Cran, you know. Besides, I want the experience of having a baby, being a mother, the whole thing."

At this point the wife would have interrupted probably to point out that she was a fool but the girl hurried on.

"I can afford it. Cran gave me some money and I have some of my own. I can pay."

So what was the problem, other than that Cran was gone? If she could pay the tab and was willing to bear the pain and responsibility, why her hesitancy? If she wanted me to deliver the baby, why didn't she just come out and say so?

They say great minds run in the same channel so, naturally, the wife asked, "Did you want Dr. Farlin to deliver the baby, my dear?"

"Yes, I think so - but that's not all. There's something else."

"What else?"

At my question, she turned and looked directly at me – a penetrating stare. "Don't you feel it?" she whispered.

"Feel what?"

"That Cran was murdered?"

The wife and I stared back. I'd swear that it was suddenly so quiet in there that we could hear the electric clock tick. "Tick, tick!" it said. "Murder, murder!" it said. "Tick, tick!

Times like that I'm slow to respond - not slow-witted, mind you - just slow to digest the meanings, the insinuations, of the words.

Nothing slow about the wife. She shot me a glance that said, "Don't tell her!" as plain as day. Aloud, she asked, "Why, my dear! Whatever would make you think that?"

"Because Cran was alive. He was happy. He knew about the baby. I had told him. Only two nights before I told him. And he intended to be a father to him - legal and all. I know he did."

Her face took on a kind of tender, far-away expression.

"I remember he put his hand here on my

stomach and he said, "For this little one I'm going to be sober, a good father," and he meant it. It seemed like a kind of promise - almost as though he was dedicating himself to us. And he would have been. I know it. He would have been." Big tears gathered in her eyes, not running yet, just lying there, glistening.

If she was lying she was doing an uncommon good job of it. I believed every word.

"Oh, Dr. Farlin!" Now the tears were beginning to flow. "Cran told me that if I ever needed help I should come to you. So help me. Please." She was sobbing, rubbing at the tears.

Poor thing! How could I be hard hearted at a time like that?

"There, there, my dear." I felt fatherly and sympathetic and pompous as hell. "We haven't signed off on Cran's death. If he was murdered we will find the killer. We're not going to let a murderer run free."

She looked at me skeptically for a moment then nodded and mopped at the tears.

I could hardly hear her response muffled as it was. "Please - - - " then, "Don't tell anyone. - Cranahans would make trouble."

Indeed they would. They would see that fortune cut into by a brat conceived by their father and a bitch that had horned in for the goodies.

"O.K. Come on, stop crying. I'll take care of it. If someone killed Cran he'll pay, believe me!" A crying lady can make me promise most anything.

It was miraculous the way those tears disappeared. Her cheeks were still wet and shiny and her eyes were red but she bloomed with a tremulous smile that was like the sun shining up a rainbow after a storm. No wonder Cran had taken to her - - - if he had.

CHAPTER FIVE

Doc:

Funny what one can hear through an open vent. There was a barbershop next door - in fact, it was in the same building as my office - but the only opening between the two places was a damn vent which sometimes made for unexpected and interesting listening. The barber often knew more about my patient's symptoms than I did and my patients got an earful of gossip they might not otherwise have learned.

Wonder why it is? People, when they are sitting in a physician's reception room, become confidential as hell with anyone within hearing distance. Mothers talk about the kid's fever, women mention their periods without turning a hair and the old folks as often as not get in a good word about constipation as though it's some kind of badge for good behavior proving that they've led a good and virtuous life of hard work and chancy play. And in the barber shop the men have all the dope on who is shacking up with whom, which brother has the still out in the hills and how good his product is, what property has changed hands lately, what young buck is going to get himself in trouble if he doesn't watch it - things like this, interesting things that keep a person well informed.

It wasn't often that I had a chance to sit under the vent but one day during a dry spell I picked up a magazine article that I had been saving and settled down for a little informative rest. It became more informative than I'd expected.

'That reminds me of the time Maddie Gordon was arrested," I heard. "You remember her, don't you?"

"Yeah, sure. Isn't she the one they called "Flower"? Used to trade a lay for a drink?"

'That's the one. Busiest whore in town. Well, one Saturday in the summer of '38 - or was it '39? - along in the afternoon, (hot as hell that day, I remember), I saw her weaving across the intersection of Main and Front Streets probably on her way to Cracker's for another beer. She was staggering all over the place drunk as a skunk and trying to look dignified as old Parson Perfect. Old Kale, Kale Riley's pa, was town Marshall in those days and he made it a habit to keep an eye on the old girl.

Sure enough he saw her floundering around in the middle of the traffic and decided that it was time to lock her up and let her dry out for a while."

"Isn't she the one who always wore the dress with big orange and purple flowers all over it?"

There must have been three or four men in the room and they were all taking part in the conversation.

"Yeah. About two yards around the seat. Remember? And the neck - It had lace ruffles around the neck - made her face, red as it was, look like it was sprouting out of a ring of dirty snow - and she always wore high-heeled red shoes with gold buckles, all run over to the outside. They made her walk bowlegged."

"Sure. I remember. My mother used to talk about her in whispers."

"Do you guys want to hear this story or not?"

"Yeah, sure!"

" 'Course we do."

"Shut up, then, and quit interrupting! --- Well, she was weaving across the street through the crowds of people and old Kale saw her and sauntered over, took hold of her arm and said, 'O.K., Flower. Let's go get a little rest.'"

"She knew what that meant. She'd been in that jail before".

"Can't, Kale. I gotta go," she said. She tried to walk around him and would have tumbled if he hadn't held her up."

"Now, come on Flower. You're holding up traffic. Come on, let's go'. He tugged at her arm, trying to get her started."

"Of course by this time people were stopping to watch the show and traffic was backing up all four ways from the intersection."

"'No! I ain't going!' And damned if she didn't sit down, bottom down on that hot pavement right there in the middle of the whole she-bang."

"Well, Old Kale stood over her for a minute or two with his hands on his hips kind of looking the situation over in an aggravated manner, looked at her, looked at the traffic jam, looked at the people and couldn't resist. He simply bent over, grabbed hold of her heels and began to drag her across the street. Well naturally she tried to keep from going. Her legs were kicking - but Kale just hung on - and she was getting a good dose of pebble scratches on her fat backsides and she was

crying and everyone on the block heard her holler, "You stop that, you son-of-a-bitch, Kale Riley! You're 'a hurtin' my reputation!'"

I laughed so hard they heard me through the vent so the conversation quieted for a while and I went back to my reading not at all bothered by the friendly conversational buzz. It was a pleasant enough sound to read by - one that will almost lull you to sleep. In fact I suppose I dozed a bit because when they mentioned her name, I thought for a moment that I was dreaming.

"- - - Canody Pederson. They say she moved into the Smith Apartments. She sure is a looker!"

"Yeah. Whoee! I saw her yesterday. With a figure like that, what's she doing here?"

"Minda Smith says that she's wearing an

emerald on her engagement finger - a real knockout. Maybe she's fair game, Rocky. I'm surprised you haven't already been nosing around."

"Oh, I know her all right." I recognized Rocky's voice. "Can't let a chick like that get away!"

So, I thought with surprise, Miss Pederson has moved into town - and she knows the sheriff already. I wonder if she gave him the same song and dance she gave us? Or maybe she's trying to pump him for information. Could be she would complicate matters and, I realized with scary suddenness, she might find herself in real danger if she goes poking around for clues to murder.

ROCKY:

Oh, yes. I knew Canody Pederson. She was a pain in the ass. Not only did I have to listen to her tale of woe every few days but I also had to worry about her and try to keep her out of trouble.

Probably, she wouldn't have been quite such a bother if she hadn't been so good looking. When she first looked me up after she had talked to Doc, her pregnancy was not noticeable but everyone noticed that where I was she seemed to be also. I'd stop for coffee; she'd sit down beside me. I'd be on duty in the patrol car; she followed me. I'd stop at the station; she'd park her car beside it. I was single; she was pretty; people talked. She was a damned nuisance.

But though I couldn't admit it to her, I

tended to agree that Cranahan's death had not been accidental. Nevertheless, I resented having to keep an eye on her.

I'll have to admit that when I first heard her tale, I felt sorry for her not because she was pregnant but because she seemed broken hearted. There was no question in my mind but that she had loved Crannahan - though I wondered how she could have - but the case was closed and what investigating I was doing by that time was strictly incidental and on my own time. I didn't want to spend it providing protection for her. When she wasn't under my feet she was wandering around Cran's farm alone and there was danger there, everything from broken bones to snake bite to Lord knew what.

At first, I tried to ease her worry by showing

her Cran's home and other scenic areas of his property, trying to convince her that it was a peaceful place, not a likely site for murder. I should have known better.

"I thought he died in an old two-story house," she said.

"Well, yes, but you don't want to go there; there's nothing to see."

"Oh, come on. Please."

I refused but a few days later she went alone and when she returned she was more upset than ever.

"How can you?" she asked. "Obviously, Cran found someone else in that house. How could you ignore that? How could you?"

I'll never forget the expression on her face, incredulous, angry, accusing.

She was hurting, no doubt about it, but this struggling over the rocks and brush on the fool hunt she was into had to be stopped. Maybe, I thought, Doc could talk to her - and that's when I met Gretchen.

Precious Gretchen.

CHAPTER SIX

Doc:

It's funny how the word spreads. Like a fire in broom sedge. It seems to speed along with the wind of excitement pursuing it. People watch the damage being done and one or two might try to stop it but mostly they just stay in the background to see what will happen - who will be hurt.

But not this time. This time when the news appeared in the newspaper about the suit being brought by the Crannahan heirs against our banker, E. Lawrence Kennedy, over the mineral rights where the iron miners were working, most everyone lined up with E.L. not because he was such a favorite in these parts but because Ozarkians are just naturally suspicious of outsiders, especially those who refuse to speak our language. E.L. was just like any other banker, always out for the fast buck. Ordinarily he was not too favored in these parts but against the likes of Cranahan's snooty daughter and worthless son the local populace lined up solidly behind him every one of them deciding all of a sudden that he was a soul brother threatened by a passel of snakes. Besides in this case they were smart enough to realize that if Cranahan won the case all that money would disappear from this region never to be seen again. Well, naturally, we wanted to keep it where we might have had a slim chance of getting our hands on a little of it.

I remember when the ruckus first started. It all began when the drill teams came into this part of the County, drilling here and there for a smell of iron ore in large enough quantity to pay to mine it. Everyone was excited because, suddenly, it looked as though there might be an outside chance of some unexpected revenue coming our way. Lord knows the people in these hills need all the help they can get in that direction. Those of us who had a little land began to have visions of wealth untold without having to turn a hand to earn it. There is nothing on this earth we like better.

So the drillers came, looked around, and damned if they didn't find a whopping big vein running right through Cranahan's farm. Well, Cran was rejoicing. Hallelujah! Amen! But when the time came to sign the papers with a little money changing hands, lo and behold,

E.L. came up with a claim to the mineral rights on all the river and Hunter's Creek area including Cran's. Well, naturally, Cran raved and screamed and threatened to sue and cussed out the banker nearly every time he saw him but he finally became convinced that there wasn't much he could do about it. He'd bought the place, he told me, without knowing that the mineral rights were of any value so he had ignored not having the title to them in his abstract. Oh, he had been warned, he said, but hell! There hadn't been any mining done in these parts in the past eighty years. Who would have dreamed that those rights were that important? After all, the ore was low-grade and not too long ago hardly worth the cost of mining, shipping and processing. Only during the middle fifties had the prices raised enough to make the mining worthwhile. So Cran had simply ignored the warning - dismissed it from his mind. That turned out to be a mistake that nipped him right where it hurt:--- in the pocket.

How had E.L. managed to buy the rights? It was this way: Back in the 1800's when this area was first settled and railroads were stretching across the country iron ore was one of its prime assets so speculators had come in, bought the rights in return for some fast cash, and simply held on. After the railroad lines were completed, demand fell and since the quality of local ore was inferior the rights had turned out to be worthless but perhaps to their heirs, the rights could mean money in the bank. One way or another. E.L. had been right smooth. After WW2, he saw the writing on the wall so he had contacted these heirs, bought the rights for a song and held the winning hand not only on Cran's property but on most of the property in our part of the County. He was a shrewd old boy, E.L. was.

Needless to say, when Cran's kids found out about all this and learned that E.L. was spooning the gravy off the mines, they hired a lawyer - fast. LOCAL BANKER SUED screamed the local newspaper. CRANAHAN MILLIONS NOT ENOUGH said the subhead sarcastically. SMALL TOWN BANKER SUED BY MILLIONAIRES hollered the County Herald. All the papers in this neck of the woods picked up the story, pulled at it, sucked the juice and spewed out the mutilated remains. Those who read it couldn't have helped arriving at a one-sided view of the matter and since Cran hadn't put himself out to make friends around here the local populace was only too glad to judge and believe in favor of the banker who was, after all, a home-town boy. Not until later did some get hot under the collar. Cran's weren't the only rights E.L. had picked up.

When all this came to light, I read the articles several times. They struck me as mighty interesting especially since I had heard the entire gist of it from Cran. I'd never seen him angrier.

"That little hen-pecked louse ought to be strung up by the thumbs," he had shouted. "He doesn't know what honesty is. And he doesn't want to know. He got his damn nose into something he'll wish he hadn't this time. I'll take him to court. I'll kill the bastard!"

Naturally, this little rampage came to mind when I began to read that Cran's kids had sued; it was the wife, however, who put my worry into words.

We were taking it easy for a change sitting on our wide, front porch, soaking up a little cooling breeze, putting away the problems of the office and of the people we saw there, just enjoying the early evening peace and contentment. I'd been lying back on the lounge listening to a bird sing, watching the last reflections of the sunset disappear from the Eastern sky and the only noise I'd made in the past five minutes was a gentlemanly burp to help my supper settle in the most comfortable way.

The wife's paper rattled now and then and I remember that her chair squeaked as she rocked.

"I wonder if E.L. could have killed Crannahan."

There! That was the thing that had been dodging around just out of sight in my mind. I must have grunted because she stopped squeaking and turned around to look directly at me.

"Someone did. I'm convinced of it," she confided. "He was in that old house for some reason - to see someone. He didn't go there to try to sleep."

They say our minds are two-sided - and perhaps they're right. One side of mine was fighting her suggestion because I'd finally decided that hanging onto the theory that someone had done Cran in and trying to prove it was a losing battle that could bring the wife and me nothing but trouble. The coroner's jury had decided. Finis!

Later, after the verdict had come down, I had talked to Rocky about it and he had admitted that he had questions still unanswered about the case but he didn't seem to be appreciating my efforts. In fact, he told me to lay off. He would keep his eyes open, he said, but he didn't suppose we'd have a prayer of a chance to convict anyone.

And I hadn't mentioned Canody to him - I guess I hadn't even seen her at that time - but if the barbershop gossip was correct, he knew her. No doubt she told him the same story she told us and he probably bent an admiring eye and a sympathetic ear and made the same useless noises I had made to her and that was that.

And Cran was buried. Let's let it rest!

So. While my mind was reviewing those arguments, the wife rattled on: "If a man is going to take sleeping pills to try to sleep, he'll pick the most comfortable place possible - like his own bed. He didn't need to go traipsing off to that God-forsaken old house unless he went there to meet someone."

Who could he have been expecting? And why there?" I found myself waiting for her answer and yet not wanting to hear. It's funny a person can be torn two ways like that.

"Maybe E.L. Maybe he and E.L. got into an argument and one thing led to another and – "

Ridiculous! Now she was off the deep end. Cran would have made dog meat of E.L.

"--- maybe he got so angry he died of a heart attack."

What an imagination the wife had. She simply erased from her mind the conclusive evidence of the poisoning - and since Crafton did finally hold an autopsy,' it was conclusive, a fact which Crafton never let me forget.

No. Even with conclusive evidence you can't always convince a woman. The wife had developed a whole theory about it and I told her again and again that that was all poppy cock and roses. Cran had simply died from drinking too much booze and not counting the pills he was taking. Pure carelessness on his part. That is what the evidence had proven and why couldn't she drop the whole thing? Let it rest.

The trouble was it wouldn't lie down in my mind either.

I wonder where E.L. was when Cran died.

And when was that?

We didn't know.

CHAPTER SEVEN

Doc:

Something was eating Gretchen, I could tell. I'd give an order and she'd nod and she'd rustle around in her dressy little white uniform and she'd do all the routine things but then I'd discover that she'd forgotten the original order. Now that wasn't like her. Usually, she was every bit as efficient as she was good looking - which is considerable - so when she began to fall apart, I noticed. No R.N. does this unless there's a problem.

Mrs. Clovington is one of my nervous patients. By 'nervous' I mean the kind who comes in with so many symptoms - real and imagined - that it is hard to tell whether she is honest-to-God sick. She had been coming in lately without too many complaints but this time she looked downright miserable.

"Did you take her temperature?" I asked Gretchen.

"Yes, Doctor. It's normal." And she had checked 'normal' on the patient's chart.

But I knew better. "You'd better check again."

I sat back and watched the expression on Gerty's face as she checked for the second time. When she realized her error, she took a horrified glance at me, her eyes filled with tears and she beat it. I could hear the patter of her feet as she ran down to the lab and I thought to myself, "The wife will take care of it." I had more important work to do at the moment.

"Come on, Mrs. Clovington, open up that

potato trap. Let's get a look at that throat."

Yes. There it was. Poor old girl! She looked miserable and with good reason. Well, Doc, that's what you were there for.

Later, after Mrs. Clovington was cleared away and her daughter had carted her out, I sauntered back to the lab. I was half mad, half curious, half sympathetic and very determined to find the trouble. Gretchen was much too good at her job to take a chance on my losing her to some unknown problem.

When I walked into the room, both women looked up. I noticed first that the tears were gone but that didn't necessarily mean the storm was over. The wife on the other hand looked like a cat that had discovered where the cream is kept.

I patted Gretchen on her sassy little bottom -

something the wife wouldn't let me do too often - to let her know there were no hard feelings and waited for an explanation. From the expression on the wife's face, the cream was rich.

"I'm sorry, Doctor. Really I am."

The tears were welling up again.

"There, now. Don't you fret." I felt like a pious old grandfather. "Anything I can do?"

"Oh, I get so mad!" she said - which wasn't exactly the answer I'd expected. "You men are the most aggravating mortals on God's green earth."

Aha! Man trouble! Something to do with her love life.

"Is it us men or one certain man? Lead me to him. I'll make him come to heel." I patted her again.

She jumped and shied away. "See there! You're all alike. All you want to do is pat and pet and play but you won't stand still and take things seriously." She was all out crying again.

"Why, sure, honey. I'll take you seriously. What is the matter?" I couldn't help smiling. She looked so damn cute.

Trouble was, she caught me at it. It brought fire to her eye. "You can go to hell!" she said, succinctly. "All of you. Every damn one of you can go straight to hell!"

With that, she picked up her purse, put her glasses back on and left - - - left the room, left the building, and we found out later, left town. It's lucky this was Saturday.

Astonished, I turned to the wife but I was even more surprised when she jumped on me with both feet.. I couldn't see that I'd done anything out of the ordinary so I finally had to lay down the law - after which I beat a rapid retreat to the drug store. It's often wise to let a wife cool down at her own speed. If you don't, you're likely to be scorched.

Rocky was sitting alone drinking coffee and looking down in the mouth. (Wasn't anyone happy today?)

"Take this chair. They're all hard," he said - a tired, worn out cliché if I ever heard one.

"Sure. What's eating you?"

"Ha!" That wasn't the most intelligent remark he has ever made but it looked like it would have to do for a while. He was hunched over that coffee looking more morose by the minute.

Finally, he sighed, turned to stare at the

calendar, nodded and then turned back to me.

"How would October do?"

"Do for what?"

"For the wedding."

"Who's wedding?" Curiosity could get me in real trouble one of these days.

"Mine, naturally. Mine and Gretchen's."

Wedding? Gretchen? I didn't even know they had a speaking acquaintance.

"You know Gretchen?" Sounded dumb didn't I? Felt dumb too.

"Oh, come off it, Doc. I've been dating Gretchen since last March. Soon after Cranahan was killed, as a matter of fact. I came into your office to talk to you but you were out - at the hospital, I guess - and what the hell? She is just about the prettiest thing in the universe. How did I know she was tricky?"

He had a kind of inside-looking look in his eye and a soft, mellow expression on his puss.

"And I'm supposed to know all this? Sorry, old boy. No one tells me anything. - - - It's getting mighty serious, isn't it, talking about weddings? I thought you were allergic to them."

"Oh, I was, I was! But - well, Gretchen's seeing green every time I see Canody Pederson and last night she said that if I wouldn't marry her she'd leave town and never come back and never see me again." He sounded tragic, like a guy who is living in the depths of a pit of self-pity.

"Seeing Canody? What on earth for?"

"Why, to solve Cran's murder, naturally.

What the hell! You don't think I'm dating Cranahan's pregnant woman for the pleasure of it, do you? She's a looker but she's beginning to show and Gretchen's beginning to think it's mine. Beginning to - that's a laugh. She's purely convinced of it."

"Didn't you tell her whose it was?"

"Sure. But who would believe it? At first, when she mentioned it, I thought she was kidding so I said 'sure, I eat little girls like Canody Pederson for breakfast every day and twice on Sunday. Keep them all knocked up,' I said. She's been mad ever since.

Come to think of it, Gretchen hadn't been in the office the day the wife and I had listened to Canody's story. She'd seen her since, of course, every time Canody had come in for a check but that hadn't given Gretchen any idea who the father might be. I'd noticed how frosty the two were but I'd just checked that off as natural jealousy between two gorgeous females.

"Trouble is," he continued, "Canody's brought up some points about the case that I have to check out. One is, could Canody have killed Cran? If it's really Cranahan's kid why didn't she go for a part of the estate? Another is, if she didn't do it could Cran have told her something that might lead her to the guilty party? At any rate I have to see her now and then - I have to watch her and get to know her better and listen to her. There might be something there that I'll be able to nail down one of these days, some little clue that keeps bothering me and when that gets cleared away, when I know for certain that all the questions are answered then I'll be able to send Canody packing. Until then, I'm having a hell of a time with Gretchen."

Yes. I could see how he might. Poor Gerty. No wonder she was a nervous wreck.

"Do you think marrying her will solve the problem?"

"Of course not. But I can't get her out of my mind. At least, if we're married, she will have squatter's rights and feel a bit more secure." He paused, reflectively. "I guess I'd marry her anyway. How could I get along without her?"

Well, now! Good for Gretchen.

"Does she know you're planning all this? Or is it something you've just now come up with?"

"Well, a guy's got to think things over. Can't

just jump in. I'll ask her tonight if she will speak to me after last night."

"You'd better not wait until tonight. The last time I saw her she was prancing out of my office with her feathers flying every which way and cussing me and every other male on earth. About half an hour ago. You'd better hurry. Your time might be running out."

But he got the message before I'd finished delivering it. He stood up, knocking his chair over, turned around, bumped into a fat lady surprising her somewhat - stepped on her toe, I guess, from the racket she made - and streaked out of there ninety to nothing.

He couldn't find a better girl. Besides, if he married her, I wouldn't have to worry about her shacking up with some bum who might carry her off and leave me without a nurse.

102

"Good luck, old man," I saluted him in my thoughts. "You're going to need it." With a set-up like that - a pregnant girl on the side - he was going to need all the prayers he could get.

But you know, sometimes it's a good idea to keep the little woman nervous. Keeps her sharp. Can't let her get too easy in her domain of domesticity. It's the same old game. Keep them guessing.

Rocky:

My precious Gretchen. How I love her!

I streaked out of that store, fell into the driver's seat, flooded the carburetor, couldn't get the damn car started, took out on foot and did an eight-second mile to get to Gerty's digs, burst in the door - and she wasn't there. And neither could I find her by phone even though

I tried every single friend she'd ever had. So I waited - and I paced - and I stewed - and I cussed - and I prayed. Time crawled. I recall staring at the clock, walking away, returning immediately, staring again. Seemed like eternity - then finally, somewhere around 10:30 or so (but it seemed like eternity) she walked in - and into my arms.

Dear, precious Gretchen. Yes, your mother, my sons. What would we do without her?

CHAPTER EIGHT

Doc:

On Monday, everything was fine and dandy. The wife got up and fixed bacon and eggs for breakfast instead of the usual Cream of Wheat, the sun was shining, the birds were singing, the lock on office door responded to the key without my swearing at it for a change, the cleaning lady had done a more thorough job that usual, then to make the day complete Gretchen came dancing in - almost on time, by golly! - threw her loving arms around my neck and gave me a big, fat smacker on the cheek (Gad! I almost didn't shave that morning!), waved her new diamond around in front of my nose (and it is a good thing she did or I might not have noticed it; it didn't make much of a glare), kissed me again, then went sailing out the door and down toward the drug store to tell her best friend. I didn't say anything about her leaving because I figured that in the state she was in she wouldn't be anything but trouble in the office. Give her a little time to cool off.

I was examining an x-ray when she returned. Damned if she didn't kiss me again. More of that, I might get right nervous.

"You very sweet, old dear. You good, delicious, wonderful old man. I love you, I love you. I don't know how you did it, but I love you."

Old? Was she talking about me? I just grinned.

"How did you do it?" she asked. All elated curiosity.

"Oh, I told him that you were crying your pretty little eyes out for him and he had better hunt you up and make an honest woman out of you."

"You didn't! Doc, you didn't!"

Didn't? Wasn't that the name of the game? I never will understand women!

"Sure, I did. You were, weren't you?" She was grinning at me so I grinned back. "Worked, didn't it? Really stirred him up, didn't I? Set his tail on fire and he went sprinting out of that store as if he was hearing the call of angels. Don't knock it, darling. Just be happy. And leave it to Uncle Doc. If it hurts, I'll fix it if I can."

I put my arm around her shoulders, gave her a tender, grandfatherly hug, winked, and left her there - with tears in her eyes, for

107

heaven's sake! I'll never understand them, never if I live to be a thousand.

CHAPTER NINE

Doc:

One night in early September - hot as hell, I remember - I took out to play poker with the boys, which I do now and then, it usually being a profitable way to spend the evening. There was a pharmacist, a friend of mine, whose one and only love seemed to be a king-high straight flush - and he always had hope of drawing one - so he'd get on the phone, call the boys and we'd traipse out to assure him that this wasn't the night, nor the time, and that he should have saved his money until his astrological stars were in the right position or something. But he never stopped hoping.

If you won't tell anyone, I'll tell you how to get there. You drive down the highway until you come to the great big billboard with the words JESUS SAVES printed on it in fluorescent yellow on black, turn down the lane to the right, two or three houses, and turn in at the mailbox with the name John Alderman on it. Lord knows why John lived 'way out there by himself but one thing for sure, it is private for poker. John is no longer there but we still use the place and since poker playing was slightly illegal in these parts it needed to be private.

John was jumpy and irritable but he was getting old like the rest of us, I supposed, and he didn't have a wife to smooth out the kinks for him. How come? I don't know. He should have, Lord knows! He had an awful lot of points in his favor. It's a wonder some enterprising young thing hadn't snatched him up years before.

He was handsome for one thing, meaning that he didn't have a paunch, he was a sporty dresser, and he had hair, brown and wavy and gorgeous. Furthermore, he was well off. He started out in a little hole-in-the-wall drug store over on Third Street and from the very first day his business boomed. At that time he was the only registered pharmacist in town but even if he hadn't been I believe that he would have made money because he was so smooth, so sympathetic and soft-spoken, that people just naturally gravitated in his direction when they weren't feeling up to par. He had a bedside manner far exceeding any of the local M.D.'s (including mine, though I hate to say it) and he seldom missed a chance to put it to use. His business finally grew too large for the little store so he moved it down to Front Street and there he stayed, grabbing money like it was going out of style. Seems to me, as handsome and well heeled as he was, he could have found someone to share his troubles if he'd tried.

The wife says he was single because he was just too damn stingy to pay for a wedding license - and maybe she's right. He surely didn't spend much money where it could be seen. His buildings, for instance. I don't know which is the oldest, the store or his house - about even up, I'd say - but they were both showing the wear of years, needing the foundations strengthened, paint jobs, roof repair - all the things most property owners take as a matter of course in order to protect the value of their property. But not John!

Take the room we played poker in. It's little, first of all, so damn little that we were practically sitting on one another's laps. He moved this big, round scarred table right smack-dab in the middle, hung a metal-covered lamp over it with seven chairs around, set one of those cheap plastic T.V. trays in the corner (for the coffee pot and the water pitcher for those who need water to wash down their whiskey) and a few cups which were forever being knocked off the table necessitating a scramble under it to recover them and that is all. When we got in there, the traffic was so thick that one titmouse would have made congestion.

Besides being little, the room was stuffy and hot. Lord, it was hot! There was only one window, a skinny peep-hole of a window, and

113

some smart-aleck built it clear up by the ceiling probably to keep the air from circulating in and out so of course when we all got in there and lit up - some of those guys smoke the stinkingest stogies you ever smelled - the smoke began to shift around and thicken and before long one could practically dish it up for serving. Most of the time we would leave the door open in hopes that the smoke would seep into the rest of the house instead of just lying over the table but in view of the position and size of that window and realizing how little air can get in to start the circulating, I always considered that as unlikely.

Just because the surroundings weren't of the first water doesn't mean that we didn't have a good time. Those guys were a congenial bunch, always waiting for a good laugh, always kidding one another, always playing practical jokes - which reminds me of the one Rocky played one night. I guess, since I brought it up, I might as well take time to tell you about it - but it's digressing some from my story.

That time, Rocky hadn't shown up to fill his seat but we thought nothing of it. That happened every now and then when he couldn't get away from his job. After all, being the sheriff, he had to be a mite careful about openly associating with us sinners.

Well, anyway, we were having a hot game that night. There had been some good hands, some wild betting with a small mountain of quarters on the table (we ordinarily play a quarter limit just to keep the game friendly), and the smoke was steaming around our heads as though Satan had joined the game (which some folks would say he always sits in on) and we were all concentrating, just willing the right cards to fall and some were breathing hard and the tension was built up taunt and tight, straining to let go. The only sounds in the room, if I remember correctly, were the sounds of money jingling on the table and men calling their bets. There we all sat, every one of us thinking he held the winning hand and - -

A siren screamed right outside that puny little window.

"Raid!" someone shouted.

You've never seen such scrambling. Money splattered every which way as we bounded to our feet and tried to get through the only door, all six of us at the same time. Naturally, the door wasn't big enough - especially with four heavyweights in the crowd. We pushed and shoved and got our feet stepped on and cussed - and when the door-frame gave, we exploded out for all the world, Rocky said, like we'd been pricked in the backsides with the Devil's pitchfork.

Rocky got a real bang out of that, it being his siren we'd heard, but the rest of us stayed mad for at least half an hour - until we got the money picked up. We never did know who won that pot but some tricky rat had grabbed it on the way out - John, I suspect, because he wasn't as mad as he should have been under his compromising circumstances.

Well, that's the kind of crowd we were, fun loving boys, all of us.

John was the most intense gambler I knew,

117

the kind of man who can't bring himself to judge a hand a loser then turn it over and wait for the next deal. Not him! He was the compulsive type, always hanging in there, throwing in his bet, waiting anxiously for the next card, hoping that somehow lady luck would come his way. If she didn't he sometimes tried to buy the pot - that is bet so high that no one had the guts to call him. That way he could win without having to show what trash he'd been pinning his hopes on. When he did get a betting hand, he'd go the top limit as long as anyone would stay with him hoping to win high - a good pot - hoping to make up for his losses. He had no patience for the fun of the game; to him, it was a battle of wit and luck and determination. That was the kind of player he was.

Next to him, on the right, was E.L. Kennedy's seat. Now E.L. was just about the same man all the time - in the bank or at the table. He played by the odds. He'd turn over unless he had a sure thing but when he did draw some lucky cards, he'd keep raising a sucker, milking the hand for all it would give - cautiously. When he won a pot he put it in his pocket - he certainly didn't 'leave it on the table for us to drool over. If he lost, his only comment was, "Deal! Damn it! Deal!" He was a little guy, that he was, but he was a mighty spunky poker player.

Floyd Turner's chair was between E.L.'s and mine. Floyd was a rat, a native rat. Once upon a time he was lucky enough to beget a hedge child with the daughter of one of the most successful farmers in this neck of the woods and then he drank through the old man's money, through the farm, and tried to drink through his wife's wages. He was a go-getter - take her to work and then go get her - and while she was trying to make a living for the family, he was figuring some way to get rid of it - like playing poker. And his poker playing was just like the rest of his schemes: lousy. We always had to watch him. He'd short the pot or do a little fast shuffling or (when he was dealing) try to take a sneaking peak at the cards, nothing as big as coming up with an extra ace but just little aggravating things, ornery things, that made me wish he'd take his card playing elsewhere

My seat was next - and if you want to know my playing habits, you'll have to sit in on the game. Until then, I'll keep my secrets to myself, every blessed one of them.

Marion Clark occupied the chair next to mine. He' was a strange one; no one knew where he came from or anything about him. He just moved in, a loner apparently, and though he's friendly enough, he remained distant. We might have liked the guy if he hadn't been so hard to look at but I for one was just too old and set in my ways to enjoy seeing a grown man deliberately go against the grain of humanity. He had red hair, fiery red, beautiful, but it hanged in greasy strings down on his shoulders and he'd added a pair of gold ear rings and a pair of stupid round specs with the metal rims - the kind that your great grandfather used to wear in his heyday. A little eyebrow of a mustache decorated his upper lip and a long, skinny, oriental goatee hid his chin. He always smelled nice, of cologne and powder (and when the room heated up, perspiration) and his clothes, what there was of them, covered a body that was lean, supple, and graceful. He wore his pants, those days, a size too tight and at half-mast so that they hung just about an inch above his utensil (which might send the girls but it sure didn't do anything for me), his shirt was invariably left open to show as much sexy red chest hair as possible and he traveled barefoot most of the time. I don't mean to say that he was queer in a sexual way - his motions weren't effeminate or anything like that - but he seemed mighty queer compared to the rest of us hillbillies. There was, however, one thing that we who sat at that poker table learned to admire about him: he was mighty crafty when it came to winning money. He seemed to be able to tell whether a man held a good hand or was bluffing; he appeared to know when to raise the ante, just how high to go, when to check to let others make the first move - that kind of thing. I, for one, learned to respect his poker playing, that I did.

The next chair was Rocky's. And Rocky, you were one of the luckiest players I have ever seen. Did you lads know that he can bet with a pair of aces showing and come up with a flush almost every time? I've never seen such luck. He sits there with that devil-damn-it expression, talking like he was suffering from diarrhea of the mouth and constipation of the brain, raking in cards that the rest of us are praying for. And under all that talk, he's still sharp as a sword.

Jake Kline liked to sit as close to the door as possible - couldn't stand the smell, he said. So he took the last chair, between Rocky and John and nearest the door and imagined that the air was sweeter there - he had a better imagination than the rest of us. Jake was a Canadian born and bred in the cold north who had come south to the land of sunshine and heat to spend the balance of his days just simply doing the things that were closest to his heart like hunting, fishing and playing poker. He had lit in the Ozarks, I guess, because the hills reminded him of home and he had stayed because some enterprising real estate broker got to him. "I liked the rocks and the hills and the promise of wild game," he told me, "so the wife and I decided that we had found paradise and we had better latch on to a chunk of it while we had the chance." So he bought a rock pile, stocked it with chickens and pigs and beef cattle, unpacked his shot gun and fishing pole and proceeded to live the kind of life he'd always dreamed of. So far as poker was concerned, he was no fool but I'll always think that he played more for the good companionship than for the money.

Seven of us - just the right size for a good poker game. Some of the nights were wild like the night Rocky blasted us out of there with that damn siren but (and every poker player will know what I mean) there were some nights when the cards were cold and unhappy.

This night in August that I started to tell you about, we had been playing for quite a spell starting off well enough, just six of us to begin with because Rocky didn't show up until after he'd said good night to his Dream Boat but then later the cards quit coming and the game got downright uninteresting. None of us was getting anything to brag about, not even Rocky when he arrived, just the kind of hands where a king-ten wins over a king-eight and the pot lay there, stagnant, while we'd check all around. Naturally, someone would sweeten it once in a while just to keep the game going but we simply were being dealt such putrid hands that we were all losing interest. I suppose you have seen nights like that, times when the cards have been so bad that any other subject in the world is more captivating.

I remember Jake had turned his cards over and was sitting reared back on his chair, taking it easy, watching the play and trying to pick up the desultory mood we had slipped into. Even Rocky was quiet.

"Yep, there is going to be lots of quail this fall," Jake was saying. "I saw sign of them over around Hunter's Creek. Took my gear and went fishing this morning and there was all kind of sign there. Deer, too."

"That reminds me," he continued while no one listened. "I saw a doe standing at the edge of a field of flowers this morning, the most beautiful sight I ever saw. The plants were tall, dark green with strange looking long-pointed yellowish green flowers blooming up the stem, and those plants looked so damn perfect they looked like they had been cultivated and there was the doe, soft and shining, standing at the edge of the field, her head up, looking around for all the world like she knew I was there. The

127

smell was kind of rancid but, glory!, it was pretty!"

"Leave it to you to notice a smell," someone muttered.

"I wonder what those flowers could have been?" he continued, ignoring the interruption. "Doc, if I bring one in, do you suppose we could look it up? My wife would like to know. She has gone almost as crazy as you are about flowers since we moved down here."

My hand was showing a little hope finally and besides, I'm not all that crazy about flowers. That patch of posies growing in our front yard doesn't qualify me as much of an authority. - - - Now, let's see. Two ladies in the hole and a three, nine, lady up and I had a chance at a pretty fair hand. Now, if just the

128

right card falls - -

"Sure, anytime," I answered, absent-mindedly. It wasn't until later that I really heard what he had said.

Rocky:

Doc has certainly nailed those poker players on the head. They were exactly as he has described them - except that he ignored his own peculiarities at the table. I wonder if he realizes that he was one of the most unique players in the crowd.

The rest of us dressed like the country boys we were (except Marion) and Doc wasn't a fancy dresser but his daily uniform consisted of a starched white dress shirt, navy blue wool trousers, white sport socks and black wing tip shoes. His neck tie - and he seemed to be wedded to this certain one - was a dark red with yellow and blue diagonal stripes. It was almost always askew and the first thing he did when he sat down at that poker table - like clockwork, he did it - was loosen the tie, unbutton the shirt collar, stretch his neck, shake his hands and arms to relax them, yawn, dig his ante out of his pocket, toss it toward the middle of the table, pick up the deck and start dealing. No waiting to cut for the deal or any of that foolishness.

And talk about careful! E.L. Kennedy didn't hold a candle to Doc. If he bet you could very well believe that he held a good hand; otherwise, after the first peek - or maybe the second - he turned those cards upside down and kept his money close to his stomach.

But, I discovered, not always. One evening, I

remember, I came in late and was trying to edge around him to reach my seat and I happened to see his hand. Never have seen a poorer one but from the way he was betting against John, you'd have thought he held four aces. Finally John folded, Doc scattered his cards face down on the table and raked in the pot. Slickest buy I'd ever seen.

Probably none of us are likely to forget the night that Jake Cline was reminiscing about the deer and the scenery. Where, I wondered, had Jake been? Ever since Cran's death I'd been keeping my eyes open for a big patch of marijuana but with no success so if there was a field like Jake was describing - and I didn't doubt that there was - why hadn't I found it?

But before I could ask Doc raised the ante, Marion raised him, the pot began to grow, the game was suddenly interesting and I forgot, yes, I forgot to ask, a lapse that I've deeply regretted ever since.

CHAPTER TEN

Doc:

They told us in medic school that we'd get used to the phone ringing, that the body adjusts. Hell! Either they were feeding us students a lot of guff or my body is different from anyone else's. That damn phone rings and I vibrate like a bell struck with a hammer. This is the reason why, once in a while, my phone goes off the hook - I've had enough of vibrating.

When Rocky called I was getting ready to hemstitch a guy's finger back on. He had been a mite careless and got it in the way of his chain saw and after he saw it hanging backwards, he realized that it was something he'd be uncomfortable without. There is nothing I liked better than trying to fasten a finger back together.

"Doc? I hope I'm not interrupting anything."

Merciful heavens! "I'm mighty busy, Rocky. What's up?"

"There are a couple of boys here in my office who say they've found a corpse out on B Highway. Doc Crafton is out of town and if they're not feeding me a line, I will need someone to examine the body before I move it. Are you available?"

Well, now. I don't like corpses any better than the next fellow but lately under circumstances like that I was developing a bit more interest in them.

"Sure thing. Give me about fifteen minutes."

I hadn't judged quite right. Fifteen minutes

wouldn't do it. Took me more like two hours to finish the guy's finger and clear out the waiting room but Rocky waited - most of the time in the x-ray room with Gretchen.

"I don't suppose the stiff will go anywhere," he observed.

Gerald Kelly, deputy sheriff, was waiting in the wagon when we climbed in but since he was a little, skinny guy and wasn't much for talking, Rocky and I kind of talked around him. He sat there squinched up between the two of us in the seat - I don't know why he didn't get in back as hot as it was that day - listening hard, nodding his head in continuous agreement (I had the feeling that I could have said that it was raining butterflies and he'd have answered, "Aren't they pretty!") and fidgeting, fidgeting, fidgeting. His hands moved constantly. Nervous as a virgin in heat.

"I don't know who it is," Rocky answered my query. "The kids were so excited that I had a hard time at first making out what they were getting at. They had come out on this road on their bikes, probably for a little illegal squirrel hunting and found a dead man lying on the rocks near the ferry. They said that when they got there no one was around except the corpse but one of them keeps insisting that someone had just left. He was too excited to pin down, the kid was, but the boys in the office were still talking to him when Jerry and I left. It would help if he could tell us whether someone was there but I don't suppose he'll be able to. He's not what you might call a reliable witness."

"Did you ask what the dead man looks like?"

"Of course. But it could be any one of a million guys. You know how it is - descriptions are so general."

I guessed we would find out soon enough. In the meanwhile, I thought, it might be a good time to find out if Rocky was learning anything from Canody. I wondered if Jerry, here, knew about her. If not, he was going to.

"Has Canody Pederson been giving you any trouble lately?"

"Just now and then. Gretchen hasn't mentioned her lately."

Well, of course not! Gretchen was too happy to worry about her right then. - - But that's not what I wanted to know. Try again.

"Have you learned anything more from Canody? Any news about her nosing around concerning Cran?" I could see that Jerry was

137

downright interested.

"No. But she is nosing. I see that little red convertible of hers out by Cran's place every now and then. I've followed her, but all she does is walk around out there looking for "more little scraps of evidence of foul play" - her words. She apparently doesn't know what she's looking for. Just anything which might help her prove her point." He shook his head. "A woman in her condition has no business out there in the middle of nowhere all by herself. She'll get into trouble and someone will have to bail her out - if it's not too late."

Poor gal. There she was, feeling like hell and big as a tub, pushed by some inner, undeniable urge to find the answer to her problem. It dawned on me then - and I don't know why I hadn't thought of it before - that this might be some psychosomatic thing with her, that maybe she had the feeling that she was indirectly the cause of Cran's death. Maybe it's a guilt complex of some kind.

"I'm worried about her, Rocky. She's developing all kinds of physical discomfort and she can't eat and yet - - -." I turned to face him. "Isn't there anything you can do to stop her? Some order or something?"

"Not a thing, Doc. The only thing that will slow her down, I guess, is for her to get absolutely unable to make it or for the baby to arrive. Why don't you give her a good talking to if you're so worried? She might listen to you."

"Not a chance. When she comes in, she always asks if I've learned anything more and she always springs tears when I admit that I haven't (I hadn't even looked but there was no reason for her to know that) but she sulls up like a possum when I tell her to drop it. She has a fantasy by the tail and can't for the life of her let it go, I guess."

I could see that Jerry had listened with considerable interest and curiosity but he held his tongue. I like a man like that - sometimes - but there comes a time when I'd kinda like to know just what he's thinking and whether or not he could add to the story if he just would. This one, however, was either too dumb or too smart to talk and either way he was a frustration to me.

We had been driving along B Highway, an old and crooked black-top which follows the lay of the land. It winds through the hills, crosses a creek or two, clings to the top of the ridge above the river for a way then dips down through a stand of virgin pine, up again, then down, coming out at the ferry, a do-it-yourself job that people seldom used. And there was Jake lying on the rocky bank as peaceful and quiet as though he had decided to take a nap through the heat of the day. There was a neat little bullet hole in his Adam's apple and the blood from the wound had spurted free staining the collar of his shirt and had congealed - -- sticky rivulets of the wasted juices of life.

Jake was dressed like he always was when he was out walking the woods, in jeans, a long-sleeved denim shirt open at the throat, and heavy, snake-proof hiking boots. His cap, a faded, once orange, hunting cap, was lying off to the side as though he had tossed it there.

"Why couldn't they have left him alone?" was my first thought. "He wouldn't hurt anybody." I could hardly see him around the tears in my eyes. Good, softhearted, flower-loving Jake!

There wasn't much to go on. We looked around for clues but there was little to be seen except these last remains of a very good friend.

It always seems as though criminals should leave some kind of sign - a bad smell, maybe - but more often than not they're pretty careful. In the wilds like that Mother Nature hops in and covers over her creatures' signs as fast as she can. In this case there wasn't even a footprint that we could see - just solid rock sealed on one side by the river and on the other by dense and tangled forest.

The river is wide and shallow along there

and the bed of rock extends well out past its banks. Except for some stones and pebbles, these banks have been washed bare by floods, leaving them red and shiny, then the brush rises up in a thick tangle - a dark, almost solid appearing green wall running the length of the river and it looks downright impenetrable, impregnable. Of course it isn't but it surely looks that way. You don't catch me going very far into those woods. I'd be bound to get lost or come face to face with a rattlesnake or a civet cat. Uh-uh! That's not for me.

The ferry was an ancient, wooden raft - probably built a hundred years before to bring out the cut timber from the logger's camps - fixed up with guy ropes in such a way that it floated diagonally across the river either way. It was a big, old, squeaking thing, large enough to hold a truck or a couple of Volkswagens with standing room to spare and it rode along over the surface of the river high and dry. The trick was to place the load on the back end of the ferry so that the weight would push it over the water. That way once the load was on, it would glide across, guided by the guy ropes, and land on the rocks on the opposite side.

The ferry was on the other side of the river when we got there and before we got around to examining it a farmer had driven a truckload of cattle too fast to be stopped before he'd messed up any tracks there might have been. Rocky stopped him on this side and tried to get whatever information the man might have but he might as well have questioned a post. People around here are mighty close-mouthed - all of us hillbillies are like that - and probably even if this bird did know something, he wouldn't have admitted it. All he'd say was that his farm bordered the river on the other side and this was the closest route to town.

Rocky made the bugger stay on the ferry for a while (partly as retribution for being so taciturn) while we searched for tracks on the blacktopped surface of the road but how can one distinguish a track on a surface like that? No doubt the F.B.I. could. We couldn't. When we did allow him to move, he cussed, shifted his old truck into low and we could hear the noise of the cursing mixed with the bellows of the cattle and the complaining of the decrepit truck all the way up the steep incline and over the ridge. He, no doubt, went straight to town to spread the news.

Two things we noticed when we loaded Jake into the wagon: first, he'd been dead long enough to get pretty stiff and, number two, when we moved him there was no blood under him - well, a flake or two but no congealed puddle like we expected to find.

"He'd have bled more than that, wouldn't he, Doc?"

"Of course. Looks to me as though the bullet went right through the carotid artery and if it did, it would have spurted blood until his heart stopped beating. Yep! There should be more blood."

"Would he have been still bleeding if someone shot him at some other place then dumped him off here?"

"He'd have bled to death very quickly. Yes, if

he was carried any distance, the bleeding would have stopped. If that's what happened, there should be blood in someone's car or truck."

Jerry had begun taking photographs as soon as we got there. All over the place, he took them - of Jake as he lay on the rocks, of the rocks after we had moved him, of the surroundings, of the ferry floating across the river, of the farmer and his rig, even some close-ups of the rocks upon which Jake's head and neck had been resting. Later, just before we pulled out, he picked up some of those stones and tenderly put them into a box of excelsior as evidence.

Damn! Another friend gone!

It stayed quiet on the way back to town, each of us nursing his thoughts. We were just pulling into the city limits when Rocky asked,

"Did Jake bring in that flower?"

"What flower, for Christ's sake?" I only swear that badly when I get nervous.

"The one he wanted you to identify for his wife. The yellow flower."

"No. I haven't seen him since then." This is a devil of a time to be thinking about that, I thought.

"Jake's hands were always so clean. Did you notice the stain on one of them now?"

I looked and he was right. Jake's arm was hanging off the stretcher and the hand was stained. Well, now.

"What do you think it is?" I asked.

"I'm wondering if green marijuana doesn't leave a mark like that."

CHAPTER ELEVEN

Doc:

I guess Rocky decided that it was up to him to tell Jake's wife what had happened - and besides, maybe he wanted to see her reaction. Anyway, he's the one who was with her when I arrived.

"The poor woman has gone all to pieces, Doc," he told me when he met me in the yard. "You'd better give her a shot of something to quiet her down."

I could tell that he was truly worried; his black hair was all rumpled, sweat was trickling down through the frown furrows on his forehead and his eyes held a hopeless and desperate expression like a man who had suddenly realized that he had bit off more than he could handle.

Inside, Karen Kline was lying face down on the couch. Poor thing! Her whole body was shaking with grief and shock.

I laid my hand on her shoulder. "Come on, Karen. Can you sit up?"

She felt cold and stiff and the flesh jerked along the length of her arm at my touch. My hand shook a trifle as I injected a shot of Demerol; until that moment, I hadn't realized how close to the surface my own emotions lay.

In spontaneous reaction I snarled at Rocky. "Get out of here, man! Go make a pot of coffee. Strong and black. You can find the stuff in the kitchen. Go on, damn it!" But I hadn't any right to take my anger out on him. "Give her time to settle down," I added, more reasonably, "and give yourself a break. She'll be all right."

He hesitated for a moment but there must have been iron still lingering in my glance so with another worried look at Karen he turned and disappeared through the kitchen door.

Slowly Karen's sobs diminished but she lay for a long time on the brightly flowered sofa, her head buried in her arms, nervous tremors passing occasionally over her body. Stillness covered the room like a suffocating blanket.

"Doc." She startled me when she spoke.

"Yeah, Karen."

"It isn't true, is it?"

I sat down beside her and took her hand. "I'm afraid it is, Karen."

She uttered no sound but tears washed her eyes. "What happened?"

"We don't know yet. We'll have to work on it. Do you feel like talking to Rocky now? He has some questions and perhaps your answers will help."

Rocky had been patiently waiting and now he offered her a cup of black coffee. I noticed that when she accepted it, she held it steady.

"Yes." Her answer was hesitant and the tears were wet on her cheeks. She stood up carrying her cup and walked toward the window, the one looking out on the beautiful flower garden. There were roses shining in the midday sun.

"Yes, it might help," she repeated, almost in a whisper, composed now, determined, cooperative, but there remained a shadow of confused disbelief and incomprehension in her eyes.

Rocky walked across the room to her - he

walks light on his feet, like a cat - took her hand, led her back to the couch and sat down beside her. He looked at her with sympathy but deeper there was a searching expression as though he figured that he might find out more if he could read inside her soul.

"Now, Mrs. Kline. I'll try to be as brief as possible. What time did Jake get up this morning?"

"I don't know. He came in and kissed me just before he left but I don't know the time. Let's see. I got up at eight fifteen - but I had gone back to sleep after he left."

"You didn't fix his breakfast?"

"No. He always has cereal and coffee. His dishes were in the sink when I went into the kitchen this morning.

"So he did eat?"

"Yes."

"Did he tell you where he was going?"

"No. He doesn't usually. He just likes to go out walking through the woods in the early morning. He says that the animals and God have a meeting just at daybreak and he likes to be there."

"He does?"

"Yes. Whenever the weather is nice. And sometimes in the fog or drizzle. Yes. Nearly always."

"I didn't know that." He paused, then asked, "Was there anything about this morning's hike that seemed different? Did he mention any certain place or make any special preparation?"

Her answer was slow to come. "No."

"Did he ever talk about these walks to anyone besides you?"

"I suppose so. He was always telling something about the things he had seen. There was nothing secretive about them."

"He just walked? No hunting or fishing?"

"Well, sometimes. But lately it has been poor fishing because the river is so low. And he doesn't care to hunt until the winter."

"Do you know if he carried a gun or fishing gear with him today?"

"I don't know." She glanced across the room at the gun cabinet then back at Rocky. "There aren't any guns missing. They're all in the cabinet. I don't know anything about the fishing tackle. I wouldn't know if there's anything missing there."

"Did he always keep all his guns in that cabinet? Pistols and all?"

"I think so. That is all except the pistol in the drawer of the night table in our bedroom."

"Will you see if it is there now? Please."

"Of course. I know it is. I saw it yesterday." We both trailed after her across the room and into the cheerful bedroom and she walked straight to the small table beside the unmade bed, opened the drawer and peered in. "Here it - - -" and then she stopped. We could see over her shoulder that there was no gun there. The drawer contained only a couple of pencils, a note pad and some bottles of pills. She turned around and her eyes searched the room. "But I know it was there," she said as though to herself. "Where did I put it?"

Rocky looked up quickly from his

examination of the things in the drawer, quickly enough to see the puzzled expression on her face. "Where did you put it? You had it, then, Mrs. Kline?"

"Well, yes. Yes, I had it - yesterday. I- was cleaning - - - it was in the drawer - - - I'm sure I put it back --" But there was doubt in her expression.

"And your husband came back into the bedroom before he left this morning?"

"Yes, he kissed ---" With that, she broke down and her hand reached toward the bed where she had been sleeping, warm and content, when he had kissed her goodbye.

"And he could have picked up the pistol while he was here?" Rocky probed, relentlessly.

She nodded, unable to talk, and turned

miserably to me, stepping within the circle of my arms, wetting down my necktie with her tears. Poor thing.

Maybe changing the subject would help. "Karen," I asked, trying to be as gentle as I knew, "has Jake said anything lately about the things he has seen on these early morning jaunts?"

Gaining control enough to answer was difficult but she managed it.

"He was always talking of things he has seen. Birds - he kept a bird book in his pocket - squirrels feeding and playing, rabbits, now and then a fox or deer. The other day he mentioned seeing beaver building a dam on Hunter's Creek."

"Where on Hunter's Creek?"

"Over close to the highway. Just below

where it runs along the base of Blue Bluff."

Yeah. I know the place. The creek runs north, there. On one side great willows bend over the stream and on the other, facing the East, the fragments of lead in the face of the bluff reflect the rays of the morning sun, shining as blue as the sky. It's a hard place to get to but it's worth the try. - On Cranahan's land, I remembered suddenly.

Rocky took up the questioning. "Did your husband have any enemies? Any arguments with anyone?"

"Oh, no!" She was quick and positive. "He had a hundred friends. No. No enemies."

"Are you sure, Mrs. Kline?" And absently, almost to himself, "He was shot for some reason - -"

"He really was in danger?"

159

"He must have been. Is there anyone who might have been angry with him?"

She could only shake her head. -- But I caught just a suggestion of fear in her expression as though a flash had forked through her brain and disappeared as lightening flashes brilliant light followed by a deeper darkness.

I signaled for Rocky to lay off for a bit - give her a chance to calm down -then I took her arm and led her back into the living room. From there as though drawn by a magnet she walked toward that window, the one off the garden, and the sight must have been some kind of balm to her. She regained her composure - the quiet beauty that had always shown like a lighted lamp from her person. Jake would have appreciated that. It was one of the things he loved about her, the quiet calm in which she lived.

Even Rocky was impressed by her self assurance as she turned back into the room and said, "I'm sorry, gentlemen. I don't know anything more. Jake got up this morning and went out to see the day break. That's all I know." In spite of her control her eyes filled again with tears but the quiet remained.

Rocky opened his mouth with the beginning of another question but she had turned back to the window. It was as though she had drawn far away from us.

The sun was hot on the garden of roses.

Rocky:

Karen Kline. I wasn't one to panic but Karen
Kline brought me closer than anyone else ever
has.

What did I think I was doing banging on that
front door, opening the screen and walking in,
demanding answers to personal questions
with no explanation at all? At that time did
she even know who I was? Did I have sense
enough to introduce myself? And did I have to
blurt out the news of Jake's death without at
least suggesting she sit down?

Well, yes, I was young and I'd never faced
anything like this. And I was excited. No
murders had been committed in our county
(not counting Cran) since I'd taken that job. I
panicked. I went blundering out to that farm,
tried to throw my weight around, blurted out

that we'd found Jake sprawled, dead, on the river bank, began lambasting her with questions - How could I?

And she simply folded up, folded up on the floor right in front of me. Scared me spitless. I couldn't find a pulse, she didn't appear to be breathing, and her eyes were open, staring. Though she lay like that for only a few minutes, it seemed to me like she'd laid there forever.

I was on my knees beside her rubbing her hand, shouting her name, begging her to speak to me when she finally moved. She closed her eyes for a moment and seemed to be gathering strength but when she reopened them and saw me, she jerked away then came at me like a tiger, all claws and hate. I had to fight to hold her then as suddenly as she had struck she stopped, her arms enclosed against my chest and her tears wetting my shirt. I'd held several women in my arms but never like that. It was an experience I'll never forget.

Eventually, I was able to guide her toward the couch, try to make her comfortable, and then phone Doc. Thank God, he came as soon as he could.

Karen's response to our questions gave me something more to worry about on my way back to town: Where did Jake go on this morning's walk? Was there a reason to go to some specific place? He must have expected trouble. Why did he take his gun? Was he expecting to meet someone? For that matter, did he always walk alone or unbeknown to Karen did he usually have a walking partner?

And where the hell was that patch of

164

marijuana he'd mentioned? Damn!

CHAPTER TWELVE

Doc:

When we left, I drove off in one direction and Rocky the opposite. He had radioed the office to see if he was needed and I heard the static of the speaker as someone answered but, blast it, I couldn't make out the words - though I tried.

"Oh, well," I thought. "If anything comes up I'll find out sooner or later." No doubt I would be called to the coroner's inquest. That's where the answers might be.

The road leading back to the highway from Kline's house was hot and close and the leaves were hanging over the narrow drive, not quivering as leaves should but hanging down - a too quiet quiet. It was hot in the car, hot and sticky in spite of the air-conditioner and I could see heat waves rising from the hood now and then - or thought I could. It was far too blistering to be out walking down that road like Marion Clark was.

"Want a ride?"

He climbed in, all six-foot-four, one hundred thirty-five pounds of him. "Why doesn't he eat?" I wondered. He looked like he always did - repulsive - but when he spoke I forgot what he looked like. What a queer duck he is!

"Thanks, Doc," he said. Then, after a moment, "Warm isn't it?"

I grunted. Seemed to me that any fool ought to realize that.

Right about then, he interrupted my cogitations.

"I've had a thought." He said.

"Yeah?" Maybe listening to him would give me a key to what makes him perk; however, poetry surprised me though in his case perhaps it shouldn't have.

The rich retain;
The poor beg and plead.
The wealth of the wealthy increases;
The hunger of the hungry gnaws at
the bowels.
The fat man offers, with reservations;
The thin receives, giving homage.
Greed remains;
Jealousy feeds on itself.
Would that man could change the
ways of men that the riches of the
universe might be shared equally.
Would that God could change the
hearts of men that love might be
shared universally.

"What is that from?" I asked. I might be

showing my ignorance but it didn't bother me much.

"It will be included in my next volume."

"You made that up?"

"It came to me in the night."

I'm sorry. I can't help being a part of the establishment. I am what I am, just a plain, old, provincial doctor, grown up in a small town with parents who believed in the Holy Spirit and in the sanctity of the American flag and in one's duty to labor at honest work serving his fellow man and in the possibility that through one's honest efforts, one might store up a few of the riches of the earth - enough to last a lifetime, at any rate.

This thing about the rich retaining and the poor begging, though, had a lot of truth to it.

"When is the book being published?"

It will be on the market before Christmas, I hope."

"Bring me a copy, will you? I would like to read some more of your work."

Damned if he wasn't as openly pleased as any child. Perhaps what I had been taking for a superior attitude was instead a simple hunger for someone to believe in him - someone to encourage his efforts. Maybe then he would join the aristocracy and take a bath.

CHAPTER THIRTEEN

Doc

As it turned out I wasn't there for Jake's autopsy. That was the trouble with the business I was in - couldn't plan anything, couldn't get away when I wanted to. Just as sure as I had something in mind someone was banged up in a wreck or a baby called 'time' or a great grandfather tripped over a shoelace and broke a hip or someone suffered a heart attack - it's a hell of a racket if you want to be able to call your time your own.

But it had its compensations. Took time to treat a sudden coronary, for instance, but it is nice to see the bugger up and merry a few days later. Made me feel like my life was worth living after all. And the pay was nice.

Sometimes when I look back, I get an urge to reopen my office - but then I think again.

As you can plainly see this had really been a lousy day. There had been the gory mess in the office when Bill Fox cut his finger off then Rocky, Jerry and I had spent the rest of the morning and past the lunch hour going after Jake and bringing him in. But that wasn't enough. No! Then I had to rush away from the office again, leaving patients waiting, to tend to Karen Kline. When the poet and I finally pulled up in front of the office there remained a couple of diehards waiting in front of the building to catch me. And the day wasn't over. I still needed some supper, a nap, and a clean shirt before making the effort to show up at the undertaker's to sit in on the autopsy. True, they could get along well enough without me but, well, Jake had been a friend of mine and I wanted to be there. It seemed like a moral responsibility.

The wife must have felt sorry for me when I finally straggled in for dinner. I've noticed from time to time that she seems to go on the theory that a good meal will cheer me up when I've had a hard day then she comes up with a big, juicy steak. (Never mind! We know all about the 'no fat/no cholesterol' theory but on special occasions we choose to ignore it and enjoy ourselves the good old-fashioned way). On the other hand, if the day has been nice and easy, we settle for veggies and canned applesauce. This, then, was a steak day.

"Oh, boy!" I thought. "Now for a nice nap!"

Famous last words!

173

I was washing down the last bite with a final sip of coffee when the blasted phone rang knocking my nap all to hell. "O.K. I'll be right there."

"Who was that?"

My wife asks the most unnecessary questions. "What does it matter to you?" Petulant, yes, but right then that was the way I felt.

"Are you going to the office?"

"No. To E.L.'s. His wife says he is having a heart attack. Probably instead I'll find that he ate a double dose of beans for dinner and has developed a good case of heart burn."

"Ha!" she answered. "More likely he pulled a fast deal at the bank and has developed a double dose of guilty conscience!" She doesn't like him very well.

"Not him," I grumped, on my way out the door. "Not him! He never became acquainted with a conscience. Couldn't be that." I like him fine but not right then without my nap.

I was mistaken about the beans. It was a coronary - mild, but painful. And it surely frightened him. When I got there he was holding his stomach and gasping for air too miserable to lie down, too scared to relax. There he sat, teetering on the edge of his chair, perspiration trickling down his nose, pain and tears in his eyes and fear written all over him in great big capital letters. But he still hadn't lost that cantankerous attitude of his.

"Well, E.L." I always tried to be jolly with my patients if I could. Being sad didn't help them any. "What seems to be the trouble?"

"That's what I called you to find out."

I love that kind. Ask for a symptom and all you get is sass. Always made me want to answer, "You go to hell," but I never had the crust to say it aloud.

"Come on, old boy. Lie down and open your shirt. Let me hear that ticker."

He fumbled around with the buttons until eventually his wife stopped wringing her hands long enough to undo them for him. Sure enough, his heart had a rapid, thready, uneven sound, the blood pressure had dropped, and even though he was sweating, he felt cold and clammy to the touch. Classic symptoms.

"How about going to the hospital, E.L.?"

"No! No hospital! Not on your life!"

Even when he was in pure misery he could be contrary. Right then I couldn't figure out what made me fond of the old buzzard.

"So, O.K." I thought. "I'll argue with him later." I gave him a shot for the pain and a vasopressor and his wife and I, between the two of us since he kept raving about the hospital, put him to bed.

He was a miserable old fuddy-duddy and I thought for a moment that he might conk out on us but we stayed together and fought the battle, him, his wife and me - and the good Lord. It always takes His help.

For a while during the night, I was alone with him while his wife slept. I was dozing in my chair with one eye half open when he began to talk.

"Doc"?

"Yeah. Right here, E.L."

"I didn't do it, Doc."

"Didn't do what?" I guess he has a conscience after all, I thought.

"Didn't hit Cran. He just fell down."

Well! Now I was all awake.

"When was this, E.L.?"

'The day before he died - before you found him. We were standing by the fireplace and he was shouting that he was going to kill me and he came at me and I picked up the fire tongs and swung them, and he dodged and tripped over a footstool. He just fell down, Doc."

"Where were you?"

"At his house. He was mad - "

Yeah. I know.

"Why were you there?"

I couldn't see that the questioning was

hurting E.L. any. He was lying quietly relaxed with his eyes wide open. No pain on his face at all.

"I went there to get him to sign -"

"Sign what?"

"The agreement. The agreement on the mineral rights. I had the rights. They were mine." He was beginning to get 'riled - just a trifle. "The rights I bought from Mrs. Lee."

This was the first I knew where he'd gotten them. "What kind of agreement were you going to sign, E.L.?"

"The company insisted that I get a release from Crannahan. He wouldn't sign! He shouted and swore and came at me. He wouldn't sign!"

I didn't answer. It was dim in the room, and

cool, and I could hear a mocking bird singing outside the window. E.L. must have heard it too because in a few minutes he began to calm down, his tense muscles relaxed, and the excitement faded from his face. His eyes were half closed as he murmured again, "He fell down, Doc. He just fell down - Just -,- fell - - down - - "

So after he'd cleared that off his chest he fell asleep and I could see that he was feeling some better.

I stood up and stretched. "Damn these patients who won't go to the hospital." I thought for about the thousandth time. But I'd been practicing in Cantor Corners long before the hospital was built and I guess that I'd developed the habit of waiting by the bedside to see if the patient was going to make it. I've lost hundreds of hours of sleep that way but if I saved one life, it was worth it.

I sat beside E.L. for another hour but with all he'd given me to think about it was a short hour.

So they had had a fight! But no! E.L. couldn't have killed Cran. The fall couldn't have killed him. The autopsy - I kept coming back to that autopsy and too much hooch and too many pills. Nothing about bruises or concussions or -

Did they examine for anything like that? Could he have had a slight concussion from the fall that built up pressure and hit him later while he was at the old house? Could he have been taking the pills to get rid of pain from a concussion?

No. Look at this puny old codger. He

181

couldn't have done it. Uh-uh.

Then again, accidentally - well, it's possible, maybe. I wonder if they examined for - - ? And Jake? What about Jake?

The questions kept going around and around in my mind. No answers. No answers at all. Just the questions. One thing for certain: E.L. isn't sure. He wonders, too.

I was still mulling over the possibilities when I finally got home and into bed, but the bed was so comfortable and the wife felt so warm and cozy - and she turned over in her sleep and put her head on my shoulder - -

CHAPTER FOURTEEN

Doc:

The autopsy on Jake's remains went off very well without me. Well, why shouldn't it? I wasn't the only cog in the wheels of justice.

Rocky boned me up on the latest developments over coffee the next morning.

"--- So he dug the bullet - a twenty-two long - out of Jake's neck. It was lodged in the spinal column. But you were right; the ruptured artery killed him."

"Any report from ballistics?"

"Not yet, but there will be. Maybe, if we're lucky, we'll find the gun some day."

Fat chance!

"When was he killed?"

183

"Don't know yet. The pathologist - Jones, his name is - said that he'd let us know as soon as his tests are over in a week or two. And he's also going to make tests of the stain on Jake's hand. It'll be interesting to learn what that is."

Today, of course, such tests would be routine but in those days, they were more tedious to do. I used to feel sorry for lab technicians.

"Was there any clue that would indicate where he was killed?"

"Not a thing that we could see. His clothes were dusty and Jones took them to test, too"

"So! Sounds to me as though all you have so far is that he was killed by a twenty-two. Did Jones have any opinions?"

"That is the most noncommittal man you ever saw, Doc. He can spout sentences a mile long and twice as wide and then when you look them over he hasn't said a word that'll stand still. He's a politician. You can see that. But a good man, I guess."

"What did he say about the lack of blood?"

"Well, he said that obviously the man was killed elsewhere and then dumped out on the river bank. Possibly the murderer had to leave in a hurry because the boys appeared. He might have planned to hide the body in the brush or dump it in the river and didn't get the chance. After the boys had seen it, there wasn't much point in moving it again."

"Yeah. I'd thought of that. Do you suppose those boys really did come that close?"

"It's possible, I guess. One of them insists that someone was just leaving."

A twenty-two, I mused. I wonder if E.L. owns

a twenty-two? Naw!

Of course not. But if he does, if he shot Jake, could he have moved him? Jake was probably thirty pounds heavier than E.L. Could he have lifted the heavier body, put it in a car and dumped it out again at the ferry? It would have been a heavy strain for a man the puny size of E.L. but - well, something brought on that heart attack. - - - No, I don't think so. I don't think that that old codger could carry that big a load. Yet -

For a moment there I was on the verge of telling Rocky about E.L.'s little confession but the moment passed pretty fast. After all, in his condition, E.L. wasn't going anywhere for a while; he'd be around if we needed him. In the meanwhile, something might come up to clear the old boy. No, I decided, let it alone at least until the report comes back from the lab. Our little conversation was just between E.L. and me. I couldn't betray his confidence - not then, anyway.

I changed the subject and wished I hadn't. "The women in my office aren't good for anything these days. You sure started something."

Rocky laughed with a kind a self-conscious, half-embarrassed pride. "Yeah. Gretchen's been telling me what a help your wife is. Sorry, old man."

"I've never seen two females so busy over nothing in my life. And the wife, every time I need her lately, is doing something or planning something for the wedding. You'd think it was Queen Elizabeth getting married. Weddings! Why don't you elope?"

"Don't think I haven't wanted to. But Gretchen won't hear of it. She says that a big church wedding is more sacred and binding. Well, I'm not going to quarrel with her about it - she might change her mind about marrying me at all and I'm not taking any chances." He shook his head. "She's quite a girl, you know."

Before I could answer, he grinned and continued, "You know what she did?"

Why didn't I trust the look in his eye? What gave me the feeling that whatever tidbit he had was going to squirt me right in the kisser.? But I bit. Couldn't help myself. I have too much curiosity.

"She went to the City Council meeting with me the other night and gave them hell about sanitary conditions in town and told them that she was sure you would be more than happy to act as City Sanitation Inspector and Adviser." He grinned wider. "And they accepted."

Blast it! As though I hadn't enough to do. How could I take time to handle a job like that? She was right, of course, the town needed checking; the job needed doing. But she had her nerve offering my services without telling me about it. - - - Talk about sudden anger!

"What on earth made her think I'd cotton to that? How come you didn't stop her? Why didn't she mention it to me first?" I suppose my face was turning red; probably I looked upset. How was I going to get my naps in if I was going to have to take on the preservation of the cleanliness of the city? Nothing doing.

"She said she didn't dare ask you

189

beforehand."

"No. I'll bet not."

"'Because you'd have refused. She said that it'd be a lot easier for you to refuse her than to refuse the City Council. She'd let the Council ask you."

"To hell with them."

The ass was still grinning. "She said that you'd carry on like this and storm around, and blaspheme - her word - and bawl her out for being a meddling female and tell the Mayor to go to hell, and then you'd begin to really look around and notice things that need doing. She ended up by saying that you were the sweetest old coot in the county and, by the time you got through taking care of the things that need taking care of, we'd have the cleanest town in the Ozarks and the city would be giving you a testimonial for good works."

Well, she was right about one thing. I was certainly going to tell the Mayor where to go. Who did he think he was, coming around my office and asking me to spend what little extra time I had doing a job the council should be doing. And for free, probably. Nothing doing!

Now that I look back on it, I was being kind of silly. The job wasn't all that bad and we accomplished a great deal toward having a mighty clean little town. Besides, it wasn't free. Mighty poor pay, but not free. And (and here's the clincher) it furnished clues which finally helped to catch the murderer.

Rocky:

Doc, you old goat! Covering up for E.L. Why

didn't you let me know that E.L. and Cran had a fight? Why didn't you tell me? If those two were arguing about the mineral rights, maybe Cran was into it with others about the same thing. Cran had purchased a lot of land; he could have been bickering with several former landowners including those who had originally owned the house where we found him.

But I doubt that I'd have been too excited about the possibility that E.L. had killed Cran. E.L. might hit a guy in the pocket but he'd have hired someone to do murder. He didn't have the guts.

Nevertheless if I'd known about Doc and E.L.'s conversation I'd have been even more worried about Canody - - - but I'd have been borrowing trouble. Those mineral rights weren't that valuable, not valuable enough to kill for.

And while I·was stewing about Canody, poor Gretchen! Gretchen simply didn't understand. In her book Cran's death was a suicide. Why then did it matter to me if Canody spent her time wandering around Cran's property and nosing into affairs that were none of her concern? From Grechen's point of view every time I saw that silly woman I was asking for trouble. In fact she was warning me again just before we entered the door into the council meeting, frowning at me, arguing, and looking very unhappy.

If I had known before taking Gretchen to that meeting that she also had a bone to pick with the city council members, I might have given it second thought but when she stood up and told them off about the care and cleanliness of the town I applauded. I was so proud of her. She made those people listen. She made them stop worrying for the moment about bringing more industry to town, about making more money. She forced them instead to start looking at the area as she saw it. That, she told them, should be their first priority.

She felt so relieved when they responded as they had that by the time we left the building, she had forgotten all about being mad at me.

In fact, when she skipped out the door before me she looked so chipper and cute that I could hardly wait to get her around the corner where I could kiss her.

Her response was immediate. I felt her hands ruffling my hair, and her body, warm, pliant, pressed into mine. God, how good she felt. Her hair smelled like flowers; her cheek was petal soft and she parted her lips invitingly under mine- I wanted to glue myself to her - - - then someone coughed. She broke away, turned, smiled and whispered over her shoulder, "Your house." That was all I wanted to hear. We crawled into my pickup, she snuggled by my side and I took off for heaven.

At that time, I was living in a rented oak-sided cabin with a big front porch, a fireplace, lots of trees and a rippling creek to sing me to sleep at night. It wasn't much to look it, my furnishings weren't anything to crow about but I liked it because it was located in the woods where disgruntled people couldn't find me when I didn't want to be found. I wasn't particularly proud of the place though so I'd never taken Gretchen there.

But I shouldn't have worried. Before I could

195

shut off the motor she'd jumped out of the car laughing, running toward the front door, daring me. I caught up with her just in time to pick her up in my arms and carry her over the threshold straight into the bedroom where I unceremoniously dropped her on the bed and fell on top of her, still laughing.

It was, I shall always remember, a weekend of wonder, majesty, fulfillment, and dedication. Unfamiliar emotions out of nowhere attacked me, besieged me, thrilled and frightened me but even before it began I knew that she was my life.

Monday morning came much too soon. I recall wakening to the delicious awareness of Gretchen curled beside me, of touching her gold, silken hair, watching her breast rise with each gentle breath, seeing her open her deep blue eyes and recognizing there a love that surely reflected the light in my own.

Nothing could have kept me from reaching for her, laving her with kisses, fondling her in all the secret places we had discovered together, burying myself at the core of her and declaring my love again and forever.

Then, I remember, the alarm rang so loudly, so unexpectedly that I jumped, swore, then growled, "Who set the damn clock?"

"I did," she laughed, wriggling away from me. "What are you going to do about it?"

"This!" I lunged at her; she dodged and giggled, "I'm showering first," then she was away and within moments I could hear the gurgling of the rusty water pipes and her laughter as she stepped into the shower.

Later on our way to town, she began to

worry. "I've put Doc on a spot and maybe I shouldn't have. He'll have a fit."

"Well of course he will," I laughed. "He'll puff up like a stuffed pigeon."

She looked at me for a moment then began to smile. "Oh, yes. I can see him," then as I had hoped we were laughing together.

And as it turned out her hunch about Doc was right on all counts. He gave her a talking to about nominating him without checking with him first, he did the job that needed doing and the city was better for it.

CHAPTER FIFTEEN

Doc:

I mentioned Floyd Turner a while back. You remember. He's the one who was always hatching up the get-rich-quick schemes on his wife's wages. Well, he died.

I never did like Turner - his going wasn't much of a loss in my opinion simply, I guess, because I didn't approve of him. He had a whole bunch of habits that I can't abide in a man.

For instance:

He was a whiner. According to him the world owed him a living and not doing him justice. Not by a long shot! He'd spent the best years of his life in the service hadn't he? Been in 'Nam hadn't he? Was injured there as a matter of fact. Lost two toes when he stepped on a land mine. The country owed him something! And then the sons a bitches wouldn't give him a decent pension. Naw! A measly four hundred a month. Who in hell could live on that? That's a fine way to pay for two toes and four years of service. I can just hear him.

He was a conniver. Always trying to make the fast buck. First, after he returned from his glorious effort toward winning the war single-handedly Turner knocked up one of the sweetest girls in this territory. I'd delivered her, spanked her bottom to make her breathe, wiped her tears when she was little, gave her suckers and bubble gum, listened with pride while she gave the salutatory address at her high school graduation, delivered all four of her kids, doctored her broken arm the time he knocked her flat, took out her appendix, sewed the gash in her head after he wrecked the car and never once have I heard her complain or lay any blame on him.

He was a damn drunk.. After their marriage her father set them up handsomely with a pretty little acreage of their own on a part of his farm. Turner drank that up in nothing flat Then when the old man and his wife were killed in an accident, Katy inherited their big place and watched it disappear down her husband's gullet drink by drink. Along about then she realized that the only way her kids were going to have enough food in their bellies was for her to get a job so she took the best paying one she could find - as a sewer in the local shoe factory. That's when Turner started trying to drink up her wages. But you'll have to give Katy "E" for effort. I don't know how she did it but she kept those kids clean, shoes on their feet, food in their bellies - good, nourishing food - and love and trust in their hearts. There's not a one of them gone wrong. Beautiful, intelligent, hard working, loving sons and daughters, every dang one of them.

As I said, I didn't like him much but for Katy's sake I doctored him when he thought he needed it - which was often. He had the strangest bunch of vague aches and pains and complaints you ever heard especially when she wanted him to do something. He'd come into the office, pinch Gretchen on the fanny (she slapped him once, right in front of all the patients in the reception room), whine at me for as long as he could get me to listen, take his prescription to Aldermon's Drug Store to have it filled on credit (Katy's, naturally) then stagger over to the tavern on West Street to begin washing down the pills with beer. I could always be sure that he'd take the medicine I gave him; after all, being sick was the best excuse in the world to keep from having to do an honest day's work.

Once in a while he'd come up with a big deal like buying a bunch of pigs, feeding them out and selling them at a whopping profit. Nothing wrong with this except that it never worked that way. He'd talk Katy out of the purchase money, buy two or three sickly, running-eyed sows at the sale barn, keep out enough coin to pay for a weekend drunk and show up again about Sunday, midday, with the sows in the back of his pickup, one of them dead and the other two staggering under the weight of misery. Two weeks or so later, first time he got a thirst that credit wouldn't quench, he'd sell the pigs at half price and drink up the money.

His schemes were often on the shady side, some of them just short of downright theft or extortion. To him lying was just a part of the game like the time he borrowed a thousand from E.L., bought cattle, shipped them down to Mississippi and sold them the next week forgetting all about paying back the money he'd borrowed. The first Katy knew about that deal was when E.L. hit her up for the thousand plus interest. Or, like another time, the time he got to talking to an old man in the tavern and damned if he didn't sell the old buzzard a farm that he didn't own, had never owned, and didn't know who did own. Sold it for cash. That time, Katy said he could cough up the money. or take the consequences.

He was a smooth talker, I'll say that for him. He could paint a word picture of the moon and make you believe, honest to God, that it was made of green cheese. The words just flowed off his tongue, sweet, tantalizing, musical, rich-sounding words. Magical, they were. Full of guile. The prettiest things you ever heard. They had to be. It was the only way he had of earning a living.

About noon the day after Jake was killed Turner came into my office just as I was trying to get away for lunch complaining about a pain in his chest and looking flushed like he was either sick or drunk. And this time, he was sick. Struck by the good, old, flue. I gave him a prescription for six antibiotic capsules and told him to go home, go to bed, and stay there for a few days. He lumbered out and I finally had a chance to eat.

Along about midnight that same night, Katy phoned me and I could tell by her voice that something of some consequence was up.

"Doctor Farlin?" Well who else, for heaven's sake?

"Doc, come over right away. There is something wrong with Floyd." Damn! I don't like being called out in a belly-washing rain in the middle of the night for some dead-beating drunk.

"Where is he?"

"Here at home. Hurry, Doc. There's something wrong."

"How is he acting?"

"He has a pain in his stomach. And he's jerking. Come on, hurry! Please, Doc."

She wasn't lying. Floyd was bent double, holding his belly and groaning. He had one last convulsion and died before I had time to phone for the ambulance. Now what had caused that?

Since I couldn't sign the death certificate without knowing, an autopsy was in order and Kale Riley was the one to investigate, him being the city Marshall and this being within the city limits. But I determined that I was going to be with him all the way.

In fact I began sweating about then the fear that Turner had died of an allergic reaction to the antibiotics I'd prescribed for him. I hadn't liked the bastard but I sure as hell didn't want to kill him.

After I'd called the hearse and seen Turner off and made sure that Katy was going to be all right I plunged back out in the rain to Posey's tavern where by phone I had agreed to meet Kale. There I discovered that Rocky had joined the investigation uninvited. Kale didn't show much enthusiasm about his assistance though usually the two of them get along fine but this time, apparently, Kale had the feeling that Rocky was out of line poking in on a local death like this. After all, he had a murder of his own to look into. Never mind about this. Nevertheless, Rocky was there.

We had decided to leave Katy alone for a while and question Posey first. After all, Turner had spent most of the afternoon and evening in Posey's tavern. We knew. Kale had seen him there. I for one wouldn't be at all conscience stricken about making Posie sweat a little, answering questions in the middle of the night. If it weren't for the likes of him Katy wouldn't have so much trouble.

Posey was testy about letting us in at that hour. He'd fixed up living quarters in the back of the place - nice they were, too - but he made it an iron clad rule (so he said) never to let anyone in after closing hours and this, of course was well past. How come we didn't have business that'd wait until morning?

But being testy didn't do him a lot of good. Kale outshouted him and said that if he wouldn't cooperate he'd find himself right in the middle of a possible murder rap. If he knew what was smart he'd talk to us, now! That little argument opened the door and we didn't get any more sass out of him.

"I tell you," Posey kept saying, "he came into the tavern around a quarter 'till one this afternoon and he stayed until about nine thirty. He looked kinda green around the gills when he came in and he said that he'd been to see you, Doc, and that he had some pills that he was supposed to take one every four hours and would I help him to remember to take them. But he didn't need help remembering. He took them about every three hours and when I asked him what was the hurry, he said that he felt like hell and that if one every four hours would cure him, then one every three hours ought to cure him faster. He took the first one right after he came in here. Let me see: at one, then again around four, and the last a little after six thirty. That's right! That's when he took them. Along about nine o'clock, he ran out of money, he was getting hard to handle and I was sick of listening to him so I told him to hurry home so he could take his next pill on time."

"Did you see the medicine?" Rocky asked.

"Yeah. Capsules. White ones with a blue stripe around the middle."

That was them all right.

Rocky and Kale kept asking questions like 'Did Turner eat supper?' and since he ate at Posey's, 'What kind of sandwich?' and 'What time did he eat?' but by that time, I was beginning to be so petrified with worry that I didn't do much listening.

I had worried ever since I started in practice about this one thing. You know how it is. When you get out of medic school you're all fired up with the hope that you'll be able to

211

cure every disease the human race can manufacture. You know just what each chemical is for, all the effects and side effects of each drug, how it can help, where the dangers lie - all about it. You study cadavers and physiology, and pathology, and psychology, and technology, - you name it. You work through the clinic trying to help the needy and getting valuable experience. You deliver babies in homes (at least, we did in my day). Work, study, worry, cram for exams, - - by the time I got my license to practice I had developed symptoms of heart disease (which disappeared after the pressure let up) and behind it all, through all these years, especially since the advent of the new antitoxins, is the nagging worry, the germ of fear that shivers every time I give a shot. Pills, capsules aren't usually so bad because they're given in smaller doses and the allergy shows up before it becomes lethal but shots - there is that thousand to one chance that the shot might kill. Turner, of course, hadn't had a shot but he'd been sitting in that tavern, sluicing the capsules down with beer and he wouldn't have noticed any symptoms if he'd had them. The toxins could have built up, a capsule at a time, until the fourth was the final, lethal dose. Damn! Could I actually have killed the man?

It sure looked like it.

When they had finished grilling Posey we stood for a few minutes outside his door deciding what to do next. The rain had stopped but the drains were flooded with water; pools of it stood in the low places.

The blue streetlight over our heads was reflected in the water at our feet and, to a passerby, we surely looked like the three muses - blue muses - having a conference about whom to haunt next. We decided, however, to let well enough alone. I'd given Katy a sedative. Any information she might have could wait until morning. In the meantime, we knew, Doc Crafton was doing the autopsy. Of course, he'd have to send stomach specimens to the state lab for analyzing which would take a few days but things were on the road now and Kale and Rocky felt that they could relax for the rest of the night.

They told me to buck up, quit worrying. But how could I do that? I felt sick - absolutely sick. It was all I could do to crawl home, slide into bed beside the wife and lie there all night. Worrying in my heart, I was. Dear God!

Rocky:

I really felt sorry for Doc that night. It looked like that good-for-nothing son of a gun Floyd Turner had put him in a terrible spot. I was reasonably sure that he couldn't be accused of deliberate murder but who knew what kinds of charges the Prosecuting Attorney might come up with. And if Doc was safe there would he also be considered innocent by the State Licensing Board? Could he lose his license? Or his freedom? Or his life? I didn't think so, but what did I know'?

And even if the cause of Turner's death was kept secret, even if no accusations were brought, Doc would know and how could a conscientious physician like him continue to write prescriptions, how could he keep confidence in his own judgment, after losing a patient in that manner?

I won't say that I was as worried as Doc was but I was certainly sympathetic. Poor man! And to get in trouble over a no good bum like that - - -

CHAPTER SIXTEEN

Doc:

Friday was a slow day in the office. The weather was hot and sticky - the kind of day that encourages people to move as little as possible to keep from working up a sweat, the kind of day when seventy-five per cent of the population may be found down on the river hunting a breeze instead of getting the work done. I remember standing in the doorway, looking numbly out at the sun-glazed street, wishing I could hide when Kale and Rocky appeared.

I thought, "Well, here it comes! They should have the report by now." I braced myself for the final judgment.

"Hello, you son-of-a-gun! Go change your

clothes! We're going fishing."

Like hell I was.

They were both grinning. Slowly, it dawned on me; they were grinning from ear to ear.

Rocky came bounding up the steps, threw his arms around my neck and whacked me on the back - he was practically jumping up and down.

"Come on, old topper! You don't have to worry. Let's go fishing."

I guess my expression was something to see because they both hawed and grabbed my hands and started pumping them. I had to look to Kale for the full explanation, though, because Rocky was too full of gladness to get it out.

"You didn't kill Turner, Doc. The lab report

just came in. Turner died of cyanide poisoning. Somehow, the stupid idiot got enough cyanide to kill a regiment. It wasn't you, Doc. Rest assured. It wasn't you."

I don't like grown men who cry - it's a sign of weakness that repels me - but I felt like crying of release, of thankfulness, of pure, unadulterated gratefulness to the powers that be - to the power which watches over my destiny and which now seemed to have saved me from a horror which will never again completely disappear.

CHAPTER SEVENTEEN

Doc:

Those guys shouldn't have gone fishing. They should have been knocking themselves out trying to find the rat that was pushing the cyanide. But maybe they felt like I did - that Katy might have done it and if that was the way of it, none of us was in a hurry to face the issue. Poor gal! Maybe she'd taken all she could stand.

So we went fishing.

I tried to get more information out of them before we left the office but nothing doing. It was too hot to work, too hot to think, too hot to remember they told me. And too hot for me to be doing all that worrying. It was relaxing time now.

Well, I'm not one to argue against such formidable odds, especially about taking a recess from the office once in a blue moon, so I left things in the wife's capable hands, grabbed my sunscreen and dark glasses, and started out the door. The phone rang. Damn!

"Doc? Ben Stover here. Doc, I've been cleaning out a drain behind Alderman's Drug Store and I pulled out some kind of stuff I'd like you to look at."

Ben Stover? Oh, yeah! Works for the City Sanitation Department. "What kind of stuff?"

"Well, it looks something like straw but I don't think it is. It had stopped up the drain and backed up, so there's quite a bit of it."

"Are you sure it isn't just weeds and grass?"

"It could be, yes. But I don't think it is. I sure wish you could see it."

That was the last thing I wanted to do. Especially right now. Then I had an inspiration.

"Tell you what to do, Ben. Send a sample of it to the state lab. They'll be able to identify it a lot better than I could then let me know what you find out. O.K.?"

"Sure, Doc. Will do. Thanks, Doc."

"Yeah, Ben. Anytime."

Those guys at the lab, I knew, were going to think we were nuts sending weeds to be tested but what the hell! Let them earn their keep. I was in a hurry to get going. The next call could be something that would spike the fishing trip all to hell.

In those days I wasn't a fisherman - hence not really considered a full-fledged Ozarkian - and I didn't have any fishing gear but I guessed that if the Sheriff and the Marshall wanted to tote me along down on the nice cool river, I wasn't going to quibble. We took out down the highway in Kale's old high-axle, souped-up pickup, the three of us sitting crowded and sweating in the cab and Kale's oldest son, Jude, bouncing around in the truck bed along with all that gear. The canoe was riding precariously on top of the cab with the two ends hanging over and it was slick the way Jude managed to stay under its shade, swaying and bouncing around like it was. The whole apparatus was painted a kind of purplish pink - or pinkish purple, depending on how you looked at it -, a real pain to behold but unique. KALE AND MABLE RILEY AND SON was emblazoned on each door of the decrepit vehicle but for most of the locals this was superfluous information. No one but Kale would be caught dead in a rig like that.

Kale drove as fast as the law would allow and sometimes with the siren blasting the way, faster - a good deal faster. I've seen him flying down the highway so fast in that rig that the canoe seemed to be floating upside down on a cushion of air with nothing anchoring it to the truck except the leather strap around its middle. It was known to throw the minds of strangers into some confusion seeing that there was such a world of difference between the sound of that fire-engine siren and the appearance of the contraption but they shrugged, I suppose, and counted it off as just another hillbilly oddball eccentricity.

One of the best places to start a float on our river and one of the easiest to get to is below the Springhill Bridge. You go north out of town on the highway leading toward St. Louis, north about eight miles, then west a mile or two, then back north, through the new cut that edges Cran's property, and down Spring Hill to the bridge. But don't go across. Just before reaching the bridge, there's a rocky turnoff that drops almost straight down and under and out on the shale of the riverbed. The river's wide, there, and shallow with a nice, easy current that picks up speed as it goes through the narrows further on. It's a beautiful spot. You should go there sometime.

Those guys had the unloading process down to a fine art. Once we were nicely pulled up with the tail end of the truck sticking out over the water, Jude simply lifted down that passion pink canoe and Kale and Rocky began to stow things in it in a way to keep it well balanced yet handy.

I was surprised at all the stuff they loaded. I'd figured that all they'd need were a couple of rods and a tackle box but I was wrong. Fishing is a science, they told me, and scientists need all the proper tools. I couldn't see how a couple cartons of beer and a sack of sandwiches could fit that category, but who was I to argue?

I suppose it's a sinful thing for an Ozarkian to confess, but the only other time I'd been on a float trip had been with Cran. We'd started at this same spot our only gear being a six-pack for me and a fifth for him. The first thing we did was to float straight into the bridge pilings. From then on, it was a real adventure. The stupid john boat would swing around in the current so that sometimes he'd be riding in the front and sometimes I'd be up there, and because the river was low we were out of the boat, pushing it over the rocks about three-fourths of the time. When the wife met us at Cran's house several hours later, we were soaking wet, bruised, I'd lost my glasses, Cran was drunk, and we were both in seventh heaven. I expect even the fish were laughing.

But with Kale and Rocky things were going to be different I saw from the start. They bedded me down in the middle of the canoe out of harm's way and they each took an end, Kale in front and Rocky sitting in back, and we waved goodbye to Jude and Kale shouted for him to be careful driving that rig back to town and to meet us at Mud Springs at nine o'clock and we went purring down that river and between those pilings and around the bend as smooth as silk.

"Well," I thought. "This is going to be grand."

Ha! It was grand for a while.

There was a little breeze sifting the branches of the trees and reaching cooling, massaging fingers along the surface of the water, making it ripple a mite along the edges. Bugs floated lazily, making buzzing noises kamikaze fashion. The sun was blazing out of a blue enameled sky and the mid-August heat blanketed the entire scene. The whole world appeared to be set on "simmer" and here we were, lightly floating along in the midst of all this - God's beauty.

The river is like a capricious child lying lethargic in the sun or skipping lightly over the shoals, sometimes meandering sideways with inquisitive fingers, now and then pouring full blast through a narrow slit in the rocks then letting up again into a nice quiet little pool of silence and content where the water is deep and the fish are taking an afternoon nap.

It was quiet in our boat as it slid around the bend from the bridge and into the shoals at the bottom of the bluff. Rocky and Kale were a mite too busy keeping the canoe upright over the rapids to talk much and I was too busy hanging on but then we were flushed out into a beautiful, blue-deep shaded pool which lay like a sapphire under the over-hanging bluff and Kale paddled close to the precipice, threw down an anchor, and he and Rocky began to break out the fishing gear.

They carried all kinds of goodies like flies, artificial worms, rubber spiders, pieces of canned tuna, chicken livers, more stuff than I can name and they were selective as hell in setting up their lines. They got into a big hassle about whether this was a "fly" day or a "liver" day. The fish didn't seem very interested in either one.

Those two men sat there quiet as stone casting in the bait as needed, each man praying in his soul to be the first to make a strike. I was interested, of course, in their machinations but I was also taking note of the beauty of the place enclosed as it was by the bluffs topped with pine and the peace which seemed to descend quietly from the blue heavens above. We sat there for an hour or more, them hoping and me drowsing but eventually they decided that the fish had moved down-stream so they up-anchored and followed toward the next rapids.

The bluffs grew closer and closer together, the stream narrower, the current more powerful. Mostly, the water is deep but in places, there are rock shelves just under the surface, slabs with nasty jagged edges that can split a canoe right up the middle. It takes a good man to make it through there alone. Not many will try. But with two, one at the helm (I guess it's called) and the other at the back end (I don't know what that position's called), a canoe can be guided skillfully along the current, dodging the rocks and sliding peacefully down the long incline past the convergence with Hunter's Creek and into the wide, slow rolling current of the valley. Here's where Cran's big house is built, up on the rise, on the far side of the valley.

But calamity came long before then.

We were slicing down through the gorge, skillfully going faster than I care to remember and Rocky was singing at the top of his lungs and I was clutching the sides of the canoe. Kale had turned around in his seat so that he could keep track of the underlying rocks and suddenly I saw him dip his oar to the left to dodge a saw-toothed boulder, just dip it in, then swing it out and over to the right to keep from crashing into the bank. We missed the rock like he'd intended but we came so close that the canoe drove under some overhanging branches, Kale bent forward and dodged, and the big leaves and heavy stem slapped me square in the kisser.

Now no one ever accused me of showing slow reflexes and this time they were working right on cue. I swung around and over and didn't think until later that one should never do this sort of thing in a canoe. Naturally, the whole works tipped over and went swirling down the current and it left Kale, Rocky and me aswim, so to speak. The boat was caught further down, the tackle boxes and beer sank to the bottom, the rods washed into snags just around the bend, and the rest of the gear was washed up on the bank along the shallows. Fortunately, we'd passed the most dangerous spot of the passage and, here, though the water was swift and we couldn't get any purchase with our feet, at least we could swim and climb out on the bank.

Rocky and Kale hadn't had any such dunking since they were chitlings, and they were embarrassed to the quick and mad at me

- boy! Were they mad at me! The cussing that went on wasn't fit to be heard - The whole thing struck me as uproariously funny.

But my laughter died when I saw what a time they were having getting the boat loose from its lodging place. It had been nudged vertically between two red sandstone boulders and the current was holding it solid there. From the river, there was no way for us to release it because the water was too deep for standing and too swift for any purchase for an upward thrust on the lower end of the canoe. Rocky tried to climb up on one of the rocks to free the upper end but the rock was smooth as glass and slippery with water and he couldn't hang on there, either. Finally, Kale got a brilliant idea, climbed out of the water, up the high bank, up a tree, and out an overhanging limb and clung there, practically upside down, to reach the upper end of the boat, giving it a hefty upward tug in order that the current could set it free. I was having visions of smashed skulls and broken backs while he was climbing around up there, and I almost kissed him when he lit.

We weren't really in such a mess as we'd feared. The boat was still solid, thank the good Lord, the rods and reels were captured, and the only things lost were the tackle boxes which were probably valuable to them and the sandwiches which were valuable to me. The beer, of course, was the most expensive loss of all.

After collecting everything, we were resting on the rocks when I heard Rocky whistle.

"What the hell's that?" he asked, pointing to

a ledge on the bluff on the other side of the stream.

I couldn't see a thing except rock.

"Where?" Apparently Kale couldn't either.

Rocky had already started loping downstream and in a couple of minutes, I saw him on the other side of the river, trotting along the top of the bluff and looking over the edge. When he came to a likely spot, he began to work his way down the side of the rock (I've seen Ozark hillbillies do this time and time again; they're born that way, I guess, half mountain goat. It would kill a landlubber like me), along the face of it, to the ledge. He inched along this for perhaps a dozen feet then he grasped a sapling growing out of the rock above him with one hand and reached down with the other to pick up the shiny blue pistol lying there. Well! I'll be damned!

Rocky:

What a piece of luck. Who would have dreamed that we would be fortunate enough to see that pistol in that place? What were the odds? Perhaps a million to one? I knew in my gut, immediately, that it was Jake's pistol.

The first thing I did was check to see if it had been fired - which it hadn't. For a moment there I thought I had found the weapon which had killed him. No. Of course not. If this was Jake's gun, however, it meant that Jake had passed this way the morning he was killed. Was he shot somewhere nearby?

If we could find traces of blood --

CHAPTER EIGHTEEN

Doc:

Seeing Rocky flash that pistol around brought Kale and me to our feet in a hurry. We stumbled along the bank trying to find the path Rocky had taken to cross the creek and climb the bluff and finally found a reasonable facsimile thereof. Kale went up it like a gazelle but my ascent was more of the elephant variety. I huffed and puffed and pushed and pulled and sweat and swore and slipped and slithered, and, finally, by sheer scaredness because by the time I was part way up I was afraid to try to turn around to go back down, I made it to the top of the bluff.

Once there, I could see an old path, one that looked like it wasn't used often - just often enough to keep it from being completely covered with growth. Grass and weeds enclosed it on both sides, growing sometimes waist high except where it crept along the edge of the precipice. It was shaded by great post oaks and hickory, cool under the trees, and there was a little breeze which gave the leaves a friendly rustle.

Kale followed the path out of sight to the west and Rocky and I began searching for answers to the questions which immediately pestered our minds. We didn't talk, just searched. But there wasn't a thing, not a scrap, nary a drop of blood, no sign of a fight, no sign of a body being dragged along the path, just a lovely, cool, shadowed, dangerous path leading along the precipice.

"This path doesn't go all the way to the

bridge," Kale reported upon his return. "Goes within about a mile of it, I'd say, then angles off through the woods and comes out at a field not too far from Jake Kline's place. There were some tracks there, several days old, from the looks of them, that could be Jake's but I couldn't see anything else."

"I suppose that this is where Jake communicated with the animals," Rocky mused. "Along this path. It leads down to the river further downstream."

I'm bright, sometimes, as you can see. "Do you suppose that's the missing gun?"

"I'll be surprised if it isn't," Rocky answered. "Only thing is, I can't figure out what it was doing on that ledge without some sign of scuffle up here. He hadn't taken a shot at anything. The chamber is full."

Kale was poking around in the weeds just at the edge of the bluff. "Look's to me as if he almost lost his footing along here and maybe one leg slipped over the edge. See here? See the slide marks? He might have dropped the gun when he grabbed this sapling to keep from going off. Let's see - - "

Kale stood there, just on the edge of that mountain and all of a sudden I saw his outside foot slide off the edge and he fell down on the other knee and canted with his whole body over the precipice and we'd have had one of the worst messes of the age if he hadn't reached up and grabbed the low branch of that sapling. Rocky jumped forward and I froze where I stood, too petrified to do anything but quail. "Yep! That must have been it," Kale grinned.

Rocky gave him a good cussing and I breathed again.

"Well, at least we can be fairly sure that he came along this way the last morning before he was killed. That's the day he carried the gun. Now, I wonder where he went."

... I wasn't about to follow those two birds along that cliff. It would be all I could manage to get my overstuffed carcass back down to the riverbed and across to the other side where we'd left the canoe.

I had been waiting and frying in the sun for quite a spell when they came back and I wasn't in the mood to waste any more time. What the hell! When you have skin like mine that cooks to a delicious, juicy red at the first touch of spring, and when, on top of that, you discover that your sunburn oil has disappeared - probably to the bottom of the river - and .when you begin to feel like someone lighted a fire between your shoulder blades and your bald noggin begins to blaze, then you get the itch to get out of there back to the safety of civilization and air-conditioning. Nuts to all this chasing around and going on wild goose runs through that brush and weeds and poison ivy.

"O.K.! Quit bitching and climb in. If we don't get a move on, we'll be here all night!" Rocky laughed.

We could have talked some about the discovery of that gun and we could have done a little supposing, I guess, except that once we got out on the river again, the boys were too busy keeping the boat upright and moving to do much talking. There was no use stopping at the pools to try for a catch 'cause they'd lost all their tackle - couldn't fish without bait and hooks - and besides, as they said, it was getting late. I didn't know about them, but I became convinced all over again that I'm a lovely hothouse plant which doesn't do well except under the right conditions, conditions like a good supper, a comfortable easy chair, a nice, cool room, good TV, the wife for company, and a soft, clean bed to polish off the day. So we moved right along, each of us nursing his own thoughts, and just about the only words that were spoken were warnings to me when we were coming to a chancy spot.

Sure enough, we found Jude waiting for us at Mud Springs. There was a bunch of youngsters there having a wiener roast love-in so he wasn't hurting for entertainment - that's the reason he hadn't noticed that we were running late. Oh, well! That's the way with kids. We left him there right in the middle of the festivities and we came to town.

"Might as well come in," I invited, as we pulled up outside our back door. "I'll see if the wife will rustle up some sandwiches and coffee." I sure hoped she could. I was starved.

"A beer would be more to my liking. A cold, cold beer," Kale grunted.

"We might have that, too. At least, we can dig up something. How about you, Rocky?"

"It's fine with him. He doesn't have to report anywhere until after the wedding." I meant it to be funny but no one laughed.

The wife pouted some about our wanting to be fed at that hour of the night and slammed the skillets around a little more energetically than she needed to but she fried enough bacon and eggs to feed the army. I hurried into the john to get a bottle of burn lotion out of the medicine chest and when I got a good look at myself in the mirror, I knew I'd be lucky if I didn't end up sick in bed. You've heard of "red as a lobster?" That was me. But the cool lotion helped and I began to feel a mite better, at least well enough to eat my share of the groceries.

Only after the food was gone and the wife had refilled my coffee cup and opened a couple more beers for them did we rare back and begin to speculate about the case.

Rocky started the conversation. "These murders are surely interfering with my sleep. Seems to me that all the answers are here if only I could see them."

"Don't give us that! 'Taint the murders keeping you awake," Kale grinned. But Rocky was so serious that instead of talking back, he only scowled at Kale.

Kale winked at me but within a few moments he had sobered and begun a deep study of the foam on his beer. He sometimes did this, I noticed, to look wise; at other times, it's a very crafty ruse to learn all there is to learn while looking stupid.

But as I've said, I don't mind looking stupid now and then. The best way to learn, I've always thought, is to admit that you aren't already acquainted with all the answers.

There were some reports I hadn't heard and in my mind the time had come. Let's see. Jake's murder.

"Did Jake's lab reports tell you anything you

didn't already know?"

Rocky shrugged. "He was shot with a twenty-two - we told you that - and the dust and dirt on his clothes could have been house dust or dust out of a car - the lab is working on that. I don't think he was loaded into a truck; he wasn't dirty enough for that."

"One thing for sure. He didn't pick up any dust at home. I've never seen a cleaner house than Karen's."

"True. So. Could he have been in some other house? If so, where? And why did he take the gun with him that certain morning when, apparently, he hadn't been using it for anything except protection in the house? Did he expect trouble? Probably." Rocky sat there with a puzzled frown on his face for a moment, then he took a pen out of his pocket and began to write facts on a paper napkin as he recited them.

Number one: "Jake had a pistol but he didn't fire it. He must have dropped it when he slid on the edge of the bluff and thought that he'd lost it in the river or he'd have climbed down after it but even though he lost it, he went on."

I interrupted, "If it was his pistol of course."

"Yes. But he wasn't shot where we found the pistol. There would have been blood. Besides, it would take a Goliath to carry a body down from up there."

Me: "Why would anyone want to? Why wouldn't the murderer have left him where he was? He'd have been out of sight and probably wouldn't have been found until today."

Rocky had poked a hole in the napkin.

"Number two: He was killed about four hours before we picked him up. That was last Tuesday, approximately seven thirty in the morning. We played poker Monday night. That is when Jake mentioned the flowers."

Oh, yeah. I remembered what I'd meant to ask: "What was the stain on his hand?"

"Just what we thought it was: marijuana resin. He'd been handling the green stuff. I wonder where he saw it?" Rocky was harking back to Monday night, softly repeating Jake's words: " - -tall, dark green with strange looking long-pointed yellowish green flowers blooming up the stem, plants that looked almost as if they were cultivated." He glanced up at me. "I didn't see any today, did you?"

"*I* wouldn't know it if I saw it."

My back was beginning to hurt like hell and I wordlessly held the lotion bottle out to the wife. She's a good old girl, standing there behind me patting that stuff on with her nice, cool hands. What would I do without her?

But I didn't expect her to join the conversation. "Where did you find the gun? On Cran's property?"

Rocky answered absent-mindedly. He'd started doodling around the edges of the napkin. "Yeah. I guess so. On the other side of the river, though."

"Honey," I heard her ask, "could it have been marijuana that we smelled in Cran's old house when we found him?"

I just sat there feeling her hands on my back and nodding my head silently like a silly ass. It took a minute or two for her question to soak

251

into Rocky's thick scull - he'd been thinking about the gun, I guess - but when it did, he grinned.

"Of course," he bragged. "I recognized it the minute I walked in there."

I remember," the wife continued, dreamily, "when I was a little kid I used to get to spend the night once in a while with Delia Robinson. That was before my parents found out that her daddy was bootlegging." She was just musing along but no one dared to interrupt her. We sat there taking it all in, listening like sinners hearing the secrets of glory. Her voice was soft with memory, and sweet, and sad.

"They lived in that big house where we found Cran, 'way up on the hill and the hill was bare then, bare and smooth, no crab grass or scrub or brush, just smooth, steep slope to the bottom of the hill. I can remember one winter when we had a big snow, we took our sleds and made a slide all the way down that hill - on the back side behind the house - into the little valley at the bottom. We had to be careful to stay away from the spring because it didn't freeze over but we'd ride, sometimes double on the sleds, belly down with the cold wind smashing into our upturned faces. We could sail down that long, treeless hill and almost all the way across the valley before the sled stopped. And when we got cold, we'd warm our hands at the fire the boys built. Frank went up to the house and brought down a huge string of old fashioned wieners and some home-made biscuits and a great big pot of coffee and we stood around the fire and ate and drank coffee - the first I ever tasted."

Both Rocky and I spoke but he was faster: "You sure there's a cleared valley behind that old house?"

Me: "Who's Frank?"

"Frank was Delia's big brother. I had a crush on him for months after that." I'd swiveled my head to look at her and she grinned at me, a mischievous, flirty grin. "He had curly black hair and eyes as blue as the sky and he tried to kiss me in the barn one day."

Rocky was becoming more excited and less patient by the minute. "There's a cleared valley? How big is it?"

She shrugged, still looking at me. "I don't know. About an acre, maybe. Just a little one." I think her mind wasn't on that valley right then so Rocky's questions were an irritation and it showed. "How under the sun would I

254

know? That was forty years ago. It was clear then." Then, looking accusingly at him, "You should know. You were there when Cran was killed."

Embarrassed, he squirmed in his seat. "It was night," he mumbled.

She relents easy. "We used to go out the kitchen door, up and over the knob of the hill and then it was smooth and clean all the way to the bottom and across the valley. The valley curves around the base of that hill in a kind of crescent shape. If I remember correctly, it's completely surrounded by hills."

"And there's water there?"

"Of course! That's where Moze grew his corn when he began making booze. The spring bubbles up at one end, runs along the far edge of the valley opposite the house, and then

255

goes underground again."

"Are you sure?"

Well, now! She said so, didn't she? Sure, she's sure!

"Once during high water, we put a small log in it where it goes under and the log came out on a ledge about two feet above the river at least a mile from the valley. There's a small spring there that flows into the river. We found the log lodged there when the flood went down."

"So that's where the pot is growing!

In Cran's valley.

So much gold on the stalk.

CHAPTER NINETEEN

Doc:

Saturday is one hell of a day to be sick with sunburn!

I'd had another restless night - too miserable to lie still and too excited to relax. The wife got up a few times to put more lotion on the burns, bless her heart, and I suppose that my tossing and turning cut into her sleep some, too, so by morning we were both edgy and cantankerous. And conditions at the office didn't do much to improve our spirits.

We had fallen into a kind of routine, she and I, in the mornings. I showered while she fixed breakfast then she showered while I washed up the cups and plates and she grabbed her purse and I reached for my emergency kit as we went out the back door. She drove and dropped me off at the post office. I picked up the mail and walked over to the office and by that time she'd unlocked the door, turned up the air conditioner and the autoclave, and the show was on the road.

That morning, she burned the toast and forgot to put the coffee in the coffee pot so we had boiled water and charred bread for breakfast. I'd dispensed with the shower because I couldn't stand the thought of needles of water pricking the blisters on my back and settled for just washing the possible spots so I wound up feeling dirty as well as sore. Then she couldn't find her lipstick and you'd have thought calamity had struck; it was in her purse where it always is. And as we were going out the door, I picked up my kit by one handle, forgetting that I hadn't latched the damn thing, so it came open and stuff started falling out and my back hurt so bad that I couldn't stoop down to recover it - the wife had to and she was beginning to be annoyed. Down town, I walked into the post office and the first two guys I met slapped me on the back. I came close to taking a poke at the second one. And when I arrived at the office there were patients waiting and a note saying that Gretchen had been held up and would be late. If she had been there I'd have fired her.

I wasn't the only one with sunburn. There seemed to be an epidemic of it - along with poison ivy, snotty noses, one broken arm, high blood pressure, arthritis and rhumatiz, asthma, and dyspepsia - whatever that is. I felt like a ball in a pinball machine - someone

259

bouncing me around willy-nilly and me turning on lights and ringing bells and clanging gongs, rolling into and out of gullies, ringing up a score like mad, a score with as little meaning as the one on the machine. What is it you get? A free game? Three free games? I kept hoping someone would hit a "tilt" and give me an excuse to stop for a spell.

Things were better when Gerty finally arrived three hours late. At least we had a little more order around there. But people kept coming, one at a time or two together or a dozen in a bunch - what the Hell! What does it matter how many? Suffice it to say, this was one day I'd be lucky to live through.

I kept listening for scuttlebutt about the police finding a patch of marijuana but it was late afternoon before the gossip started; then it wasn't what I'd expected.

"Hey, Doc! Did you hear about Marion Clark? He was arrested - somewhere out north of town, I hear."

"That's not what I heard!" someone else chimed in. "It was Jim Clark, out south of town."

"And he was selling marijuana on the street."

"People like that ought to be shot. What's the world coming to?"

"The Lord says, 'Be clean of body and spirit'; just think what people like Sam Clark are doing to the young people of this community!"

Marion? Jim? Sam? Which Clark are they talking about? I wondered. But I didn't have a chance to put the question in edgewise.

"I say they ought to let the poor bugger alone. Sam's old. He isn't hurting anybody. Poor old fool."

"But it wasn't Sam. It was Jim."

"Did you see him? They tell me he looked wild. I always have said that he could be dangerous.

"I saw Jim Clark on the street just a few minutes ago and he looked like he always does - not a mite different."

"They must have let him go. You can do anything and get by with it, these days. First thing we know our children will be smoking pot in school."

"Not my children! They better not if they know what's good for them. I'll whip the daylights out of them."

"I've been telling the mister that our children should be sent to a private school. There's such riff-raff in public schools these days."

"Are you crazy? We have an excellent bunch of kids ---"

"In my opinion the kids should be kept at home where parents can keep an eye on them. No kid of mine is going traipsing off to the city by himself to go to school. He's going to stay at home and help with the chores. Keep them busy and they'll stay out of trouble."

"I haven't heard anything about drugs in our school, have you?"

"No. Not yet. But mark my words -- -

I gave up.

Rocky:

Saturday was a bad day for me, too.

I was so tired and full of bacon and eggs and so anxious to phone Gretchen when I got home from Doc's house Friday evening that I didn't even take time to turn on the lights. Unfortunately, it was late, the jangle of the phone woke her and the first thing she said was, "What time is it?" then 'Why didn't you call earlier?" then "Yes, I love you, too."

From there, the conversation became so steamy that it took all my will power to hit the bed rather than taking off for her apartment to compromise her reputation.

I intended to get up the next morning at the crack of dawn to sashay out to take a look behind Cran's old house but the stupid alarm failed to go off, I awoke with a headache, and when I arrived at the office, I discovered that during the night one of my deputies had jailed

264

Marion Clark. The reason was obvious. He was stewed to the gills; furthermore, he was carrying a considerable amount of pot. Obviously, even though he fought it all the way, he had to be booked.

To make matters worse, following his phone call, some damned attorney from Chicago got on the line and very carefully and tactfully all but threatened me with mayhem if I didn't let the idiot go. By that time, I was so pissed that I deliberately saw to it that Clark underwent every test I could think up. Finally a couple of deputies and I drove out to check that field. It was pot, all right, but there was nothing I could do about it right then; furthermore, it was time for me to shower and dress.

Gretchen would be waiting.

CHAPTER TWENTY

Doc:

It was nearly six-thirty when we finally locked the office doors and by then, we were bushed to the core – the wife and I, that is. Gerty had ducked into the back room and when she came out she was dressed fit to kill in a figure-hugging emerald green miniskirt – short it was, I remember; showed her lovely legs – and long, dangling silver and emerald earrings swinging from her ears. Made her look altogether different, something like a sexy, wild angel. Rocky had just come in and he gasped and flapped his chin and grinned and beamed and blushed all at the same time. He's certainly going to have his hands full.

"Going somewhere?" I grinned.

"We're going to St. Louis. And don't you say a word." She was flippant and sassy and I should have whacked her backside for talking back but I was so busy feasting my tired old eyes that I forgot it.

"Ready baby?" Rocky asked.

My God! You mean maybe she wasn't ready?

She was flitting around like a butterfly. Absolutely beautiful.. Beautiful.

But I was forgetting something –

"Hang on! Not so fast. What's all this about Jim or Sam or Marion Clark?"

"Oh," Gretchen was dragging on Rocky's arm but my question had slowed him for the moment. "Didn't anyone tell you?"

"Yes. Everyone's been telling me. Each with a

different story. You're not going to get away 'till I know what's been going on." I turned on Gerty. "Gretchen, you sit down and shut up for a minute. I'm going to find out how things stand if you have to wait here all night."

"But, Doc - "

"Don't you but me - and don't try to back talk me, either. Just sit down and wait a minute. It won't do you a bit of good to pester us. Just sit down."

She looked beseechingly at the wife. Now, usually the wife will take her side in a little tiff like this but, this time, curiosity was getting the wife as badly as it was me so she stayed completely out of the argument. You could see "Damn!" in Gerty's expression but she didn't give us any more sass.

"The pot was there, all right. Just where we

figured. About an acre or maybe a bit more. And, my God! what a field! This wasn't Kansas Crap. It's the real thing - real, Mexican seed, gold. Ten and twelve and fourteen feet high and oozing resin from every pore - thick, sticky, potent, mind annihilating hash."

"It's standing, then?"

"Yeah. Just about to the harvesting stage. We have to keep people away from there until we've had a chance to get rid of it. That field is worth at least a quarter of a million bucks - bargain prices."

"Are you going to burn it?"

"Probably. Yeah. And I'm not looking forward to it at all." He sighed, then continued reflectively, "Clark, if he'd had a chance to get rid of it, would have been set for the rest of his life."

Oh, yeah. That was the other half of my question. "Which Clark?"

"Marion. He was picked up last night, stoned and in possession. He was in jail by the time I got to work this morning.'

"Does that prove the field is his? Maybe he was just sampling the wares."

"Come off it, Doc! Don't try to put up a smoke screen. We have the field and we have the man. What else do you want?"

"What's the charge?"

"For now, possession. But with a bit more evidence, it could be murder. I think Jake's murder is definitely connected with the existence of that field of pot."

I didn't like it. There were too many questions.   "Somehow I can't see Clark murdering for it."

"Some guys will do anything for money."

That's the truth, but I hadn't pictured Marion Clark as giving a damn about money. That man wanted to be noticed, wanted to change the world. He'd set his sights on better things than murdering for a field of pot, things like reweaving the fabric of society.

"Was that all you found?"

"It looks like Jake was killed there, too. There's a big, dried smear of blood in the back yard near the old road, the road that was blocked off when the highway was cut through. Clark or someone has cleared it and made a new entry which comes out this side of the cut."

"Big enough for a car?"

"Of course."

"Marion Clark doesn't have a car - or a pickup."

Pause. "How do you know? He could have one stashed away somewhere. And, surely, he has confederates."

"Leave a car stashed away somewhere? And walk? Why in hell would he do that?" (Yes, I know. It's the healthful thing to do! But if I were in Clark's shoes and lived where he lived, I'd drive.) "And confederates? He's a loner and you know it."

That did it. I'd pushed Rocky too far. Put him on the defensive.

"O.K., Know-it-all! If you don't like the way I'm conducting this investigation, you can go to hell! And, unless you can prove differently, I want you to keep your trap shut and mind

272

your own business. I'm tired of people telling me what to do."

That shut me up. I was so surprised that I took a step backwards and nearly fell over the wife. And after all I've done for him.

Gretchen jumped up, patted him on his backside, and smirked at me as though to say: "So there, too!", and pulled him out the door. He didn't look very willing to go.

Rocky:

Oh, I was willing to go all right, more than willing. Doc's questions were irritating, my headache was mach three, I was too warm in my suit, my tie was choking me and Gretchen was yanking my arm. Who wouldn't have wanted to go?

Gretchen was, apparently, on a psychological high. As we pulled out of town and sped toward the interstate, she rattled nonstop about Doc, her job, the patients' complaints, the wedding and any other subject that came to mind and the more she talked, the harder I tried to concentrate. But I couldn't; I was just too damn tired. Finally, I pulled over on the shoulder, got out of the car, walked around it, shoved her into the driver's seat, took off my coat and tie, grabbed a stashed pillow, and hunkered down for a nap.

"Oh, sweetheart, are you tired?" she asked unnecessarily. I grunted.

From then on, all the way to St. Louis, I rested, not really asleep but relaxed. The radio was playing top ten tunes, volume muted, the air conditioner was purring, and Gretchen, concentrating on the road, was unaware that I frequently stirred to feast my eyes on her.

She was quiet until she pulled up in front of the Frontenac Hotel then before I could get out of the car she said, "Let's register then go to dinner. I'm hungry."

Exactly what I had in mind except that I had to have a kiss or two in the hotel room. In fact, after the first kiss, I'd have been happy to scrub dinner in favor of immediate heavy duty sex but Gretchen slithered out of my arms.

"But I'm getting you later," I smirked.

Gaslight Square. Brick streets. Gas street lights. Huge old three story brick buildings - warehouses built along the Mississippi. Garish posters advertising coming events. Cacophony emanating from open doors. Antique shop windows dimly lighted. Highly

275

polished locked doors with discreet, gold identification signs. People, single, in pairs, in groups, in clusters, walking from one noisy tavern to another, moving from one party to another, changing partners, doing whatever came to mind at the moment, almost schizoid in their behavior.

Louigies in one of the renovated warehouses on Gaslight Square, that's where we went for dinner. The place was crammed, the noise was deafening, the psychedelic lights were blinding, the aroma enticing, the mood mellow like old home place to me. Brought back my college days when I was coming from Mizzou into St. Louis for weekend singing engagements to pay for my education. Even the maitre'd was the same.

I was surprised to discover that this was

adventure for Gretchen. I hadn't realized that her childhood had been so protected nor that her education had been so demanding that she had had little time or opportunity for beer and pub jumping. Her childhood, I learned later, involved Sunday school, tap dancing lessons, cheer leading and choir; college experience was confined to hours and hours of clinical study and hitting the books. And, of course, she couldn't get much macho training in Cantor Corners on her job with Doc.

To tell the truth, I wondered when we stepped into Louigies if I'd made a mistake. We were seated in a postage-sized booth, handed meat cleavers embossed with the menu, and served by a semi-naked waitress who delivered second-rate Champaign. And I became even more concerned when I heard a high, singsong voice say, "Well, look who is here! Rocky, sweetheart! How are you?"

Some busty female grabbed me around the neck and pressed my nose into her bosom. When I managed to extricate myself, I saw a tall, brittle, angular and striking red head standing above me. Her name? I couldn't remember.

They moved right in. 'Come on, David'. We can sit here with Rocky, can't we, Hon? -- I'm Stella," she said to Gretchen. "Who are you?"

David leered at Gretchen, kissed her hand, shoved her over, sat down beside her and offered her a joint.

"Where have you been, you pretty thing?" he asked.

My naive darling declined the offer and responded, "I live in the Ozarks."

"Oh. Down where you grow good weed."

Immediately, I wanted to get into this conversation; instead, a waitress interrupted by setting a couple of beers, complimentary on the house, in front of me.

"Honey," Stella was saying to Gretchen, "you should have known Rocky in the old days when he was singing in joints like this. He was really somethin'." Then there was no stopping her. She went on to explain to Gretchen what that "really something" really was; furthermore, she had draped herself over me like a rug.

Poor Gretchen had more problems than she could handle. On the one hand, she swore later, David had three hands and they were all busy under the table; she was dumbfounded at my history as Stella told it and she was horrified that I could sit there with Stella's arm around my shoulders, her hair practically in my mouth, and her rear almost on my lap.

In my own defense, I will have to say that I began to enjoy Stella's recollections because they brought back a somewhat exotic, carefree period in my life. I had served in the Air Force in Europe, spent several months singing with the Gaslight Trio during their U.S. tour, then come back to Missouri to finish my education. That part of my life, the part that involved the Stella's in the country, was a loose and carefree period.

I sat there, not paying any attention to the way Stella had draped herself around me, drowning in her compliments and grinning like a fool. Nothing new. Stella always did that with any man she talked to. And Stella wasn't the only person to recognize me from the old days. As the evening progressed I drank every beer that was set before me, kissed every woman who recognized me, danced my old routine in the middle of the floor, sang with the jukebox and all the while, Stella's tales seemed to become more and more entertaining and she moved closer and closer. And I made one huge mistake: I ignored Gretchen.

"And then there was THE night," Stella was saying. "Remember? We decided that it was too hot in Lois' apartment and we could cool off if we went skiing so we piled into Bob's van, rode for hours and hours, and holed up in some cheap motel."

"You remember Grace, don't you? Remember when she fell on the beginner's slope the next day and you had such a time getting her up? Remember?"

Stella was giggling and I was laughing, relaxed, wallowing in the attention this bunch of drunks was giving me.

"And she was all tangled up in her skis and instead of your pulling her up she pulled you down and you were both floundering around out there in the snow. And I came to help you up but you pulled me down and kissed me. Like this."

Believe me, I didn't see it coming. Stella was suddenly all over me, on top of me, around me, and in the middle of this, I distinctly heard a gasp, a sob, hysterical movement across the table, and retreating footsteps. I scrambled frantically to pry loose from Stella, clawed my way over her lap, and ran through

282

the pub and out the door just in time to see Gretchen careen around the corner in my car.

Not a good way to start a marriage!

CHAPTER TWENTY ONE

Doc:

By Monday I was feeling some better but I was beginning to peel, little threads of dead white marbling the skin. I wouldn't have minded, I guess, if my cotton-picking friends would quit patting it. It's disconcerting when every one who passes reaches out and rubs your bald noggin with some remark like 'You're getting some fuzz on your billiard ball, Doc. Better oil it down!' or some such idiotic statement. I got to the place where I was dodging every time anyone walked close to me - even strangers.

It's a good thing I was feeling better. Someone in the office needed to be up and at them and it certainly wasn't Gretchen. Poor

Gerty had the worst case of blues and absent-minded grouchiness I've ever seen. She just simply wasn't tending to business.

Like:

I was in my office, just beyond the reception room, when I heard her say, "All right, Ma'am. You may come in. Second door on the left."

I saw a fat lady pass my door on her way to the examining room.

And Gerty continued, "You may go with her, Sir. Second door to the left." A skinny, sawed-off runt passed.

Then she came to my door and said, "Mrs. Hammond is ready to see you, Doctor" and followed me.

I like to have Gretchen in the office. Usually she's as handy as they come. Don't know how she reads my mind and anticipates my needs so well.

"Mrs. Hammond?" Mrs. Hammond nodded. ("First time she's been here," I thought to myself.) "What seems to be the trouble?"

She was sitting on the examining table, the man was perched on the chair and with Gerty and me the room seemed a mite crowded.

"I think I've caught a cold, Doctor, and when I do, my doctor in Blossom Bay always gives me a shot of penicillin. It helps to get after these things early - - -"

Now, you know I don't really like to do that. Too much danger of reaction and, besides, the cold will run its course no matter what we do. Judging by this lady's determined expression, however, she'd not easily be talked out of it.

Gretchen read my mind. "She has a

temperature, Doctor."

The woman stopped talking long enough to breathe then continued dashing off words, all unimportant. It felt like the room was getting more crowded and noisy by the minute. "---in the hip. I think they do more good in the hip, don't you?"

Gretchen was filling a syringe. "O.K. In the hip. If you'll just lie right here and get ready." I said.

She didn't move - and the talk stopped.

Gerty was still working with the syringe, I was reaching for the antiseptic, the man was still sitting in the chair looking interested in the proceedings, and the woman didn't budge her fat bottom off the table.

So I'll try again. "Yes, Mrs. Hammond. If you'll just lie down right here - -

I looked up. She was getting red in the face and nodding indignantly at the man. "With him here?" I never saw such straight-backed outrage.

"We always allow husbands and wives in together if that is their wish."

"That," the woman pointed a sausage-sized finger at the little weasel, "is not my husband! I've never seen him before in my life!"

Well, naturally, the guy realized that the jig was up and the show was over so he popped up off the chair and scrambled out of the room. Mrs. Hammond's eyes followed him (speculatively, I thought later) until he was out of sight and then she proceeded to bare one cheek of her stupendous backside for the shot.

Gretchen was hiding her face. She wouldn't look at me. At the wall, out the window, at the woman, at the sterilizer but not at me. She practically threw the syringe in my direction and fled. Her face was as red as mine felt.

And me? I couldn't apologize fast enough. Words fell all over themselves trying to be said. I practically genuflected. God! What a situation!

If such a thing had to happen, I'm mighty glad it happened to Mrs. Hammond and not to someone else. After she recovered from outraged dignity, she began to see the humor of the situation and she left happy, her temperature forgotten.

And the day had only begun. By afternoon, I was dodging out of the office every chance I could find just to get away from poor Gerty.

Her face stayed red, her eyes were full of tears half the time, her nose was shiny, her slip was showing, she dropped things, she stumbled, she burned herself, - I swear!

Along in the afternoon, I sneaked out the alley door and strolled over to John's Drug Store. As I once said, it's an old-fashioned store, one of those with a soft drink counter running across the back and little white tables with three-legged chairs where people could dump their packages and relax over a Coke and a bit of gossip. The store needed paint and fixtures and lights - nearly everything except friendliness. It had plenty of that. John might have been close with his money but he surely was free with the welcome mat.

But there I go, digressing again.

I was drinking my Coke and watching the

people pass when Canody Pederson sat down beside me. She looked big, miserable, and uncomfortable and I felt sorry for her like I do every time I lay eyes on her. She'd been having her pre-natal checkups regularly and the baby was coming along fine but she'd been feeling so bad that I couldn't help wondering if she'd ever regretted her decision. How she could enjoy her pregnancy as she had intended I don't know.

"Hi, Canody. How are you?"

"Better, Doctor. Thank goodness the time is about up. Another month I think I'd go stark, raving mad!"

I nodded, agreeing with her.

"You're ready, are you? Good. First time you feel a pain, be sure to call me. You don't want to have that baby in the hospital lobby, you know."

Then I realized that she hadn't heard what I'd been saying and I turned to see what had startled her so.

John had come out of his office looking glum and pale and nervous (he'd been jumpy like that a lot lately) and he wasn't alone. A short, stocky, almost paunchy little man with a black beard and bone-rimmed specs had emerged with him. As we watched, he said one last word to John then turned and walked our way. When he did so, he noticed Canody. I looked at her, too. She was sitting on the little three-legged chair, perched there like a pregnant bird whose wings will no longer lift the weight, straight and brave and helpless.

The stranger spoke. "Hello, there, sweetheart! So this is where you're hiding. I've wondered." Then, looking me over, he continued, "Is this your man?"

"No." She almost whispered but we could hear her well enough. "This is my doctor, Dr. Farlin. Doctor, may I introduce Spike Gablongo. I used to work for him in St. Louis. Spike owns a night club where I was a dancer."

Ah, so! A dancer. It figures! But - for this bird?

Gablongo held out a hand, hard and heavily muscled, and scrunched my knuckles together in his grip. "How-d-y-do. Glad to know ya. You takin' good care of this little 'un? I see she's got herself knocked up. Too bad, sweetheart." he said, turning back to her. "You shouldn't treat that beautiful body that way. Your man around?"

She shook her head and I came to her rescue. This bird didn't need to know. "Her husband died (I'd almost said 'was killed') a few months ago. But she's getting along all right." I patted her arm reassuringly. "We like her here in Cantor Corners."

He was still staring at her but he spoke to me. "Do ya now! I'll bet ya do. Bring goose bumps to all the locals, sweetheart? Swingin' your fanny around down here in the sticks? Once too often, eh?"

He grinned a very nasty grin. I felt an itch to wipe it off.

"Well, good luck, Sweety, but remember when they get sick of you don't come cryin' back to me. You're not workin' for me no more. Remember that, Sweetheart."

He reached a couple of fingers to her face

and the pinch left a nasty red mark on her cheek, then he turned on his well-stacked heel and bounced out the door and into the Cadillac sitting in front of the store in the 'no parking' zone. The guy who had been waiting for him revved up the motor and they purred away.

"There's a louse if I ever saw one," I thought. To Canody, I said, "Are you all right?" She only nodded in answer to my question.

John had taken in this little scene, first looking surprised, then puzzled, then thoughtful, but as the gangster type walked out, he turned, shrugged and, in a moment, I saw him saunter out the back door.

"Well, so long, Canody. See you next Wednesday if I don't see you before then." No use my wasting any more time. No use at all.

She was staring at the back of the store when I left and didn't even see me go.

Rocky:

If Doc or Canody had mentioned Gablongo's name to me, if either of them had described that little incident, I may have put two and two together more quickly. I was quite aware of Gablongo's reputation in cities all over the country because during my singing days I'd heard his name mentioned more than once, always in whispers, always in dim, dark corners, always with clandestine drugs involved and always with a wad of money changing hands. And I hated him. When Joey, our Gaslight Trio arranger, got hooked and died late one night in my arms of an overdose, I blamed Gablongo. If it weren't for geeks like

296

him, thousands of young Americans would still be alive. What a waste!

Then again without Joey's death I wouldn't have gone into law enforcement and on into government service so I wouldn't have been around to meet Gretchen.

I was so worried about Gretchen that Monday that I may have ignored any mention of Gablongo if it had been made. I hadn't seen her since she fled *Lougies* on Saturday night. She had left me without wheels so I'd had to taxi to the Frontenac. Since she wasn't there I phoned a pal on the State Patrol with a request that they watch for her and keep me posted, called Kale with the same message, stewed and fretted, tried to sleep, prayed, and finally took the bus back to Cantor Corners.

Monday morning, I found my car parked

297

outside my front door so I yanked up the phone, dialed her number, and the answering machine said, "Get off the line, Rocky. You're dead meat." At least, I thought, she's at home.

So I had problems of my own that Monday. I wasn't losing any sleep over the safety of our town. "Damn it!" I thought. "Let those sheep find another shepherd."

CHAPTER TWENTY TWO

Doc:

During our supper, a pork chop night, the news that Marion Clark had been formally charged by a Coroner's jury of Jake's murder came over TV. They showed pictures of the poor bugger trying to hide his face from the camera by throwing his hand-cuffed fists up and dodging his head behind an arm, being escorted by a couple of deputies down the hall and into a cell where, supposedly, he'd stagnate until someone could come to his rescue. I suspected that he was short on both friends and funds and without a little help might be badly mauled during the next few weeks.

On the other hand, could he be the killer?

"Isn't that a shame!" the wife said. "I feel so sorry for him. He looks like such a nice boy." This surprised me somewhat because she doesn't ordinarily go for the longhaired type. "He has such a sensitive face. I'm going with you."

Going with me where? But then I knew immediately that I would be going. Do my good turn for the day.

"Oh, no. You stay out of that jail. That buzzard's been arrested for murder." For one murder, I realized. Are there two murderers loose in this community? Did Clark kill both Jake and Turner? Or did someone else do it and is happy to let Clark take the rap?

She smiled, cat like. Damned if she hadn't baited me and I'd bit. "I'll stay here if you'll see him tonight. What if he wants you to put up bail?"

"Depends on how much they want and what he has to say. I like my money where it is, not riding on some possible murderer, no matter how pretty he is."

But no danger. If I'd offered my entire bundle, the judge wouldn't have let him out. The newspapers and TV were having a field day casting Clark as the number one menace to the youth of the Ozarks and if the judge had been the least bit compromising he'd have been swarmed by excited reporters, angry parents, and righteous preachers. Their dander was up. They'd had the entire weekend to mull it over. No stupid son-of-a-gun was going to let a viper like that loose on their poor, unsuspecting, innocent children if they could help it. Clark was probably safer in jail. Let him out, he might be lynched.

They did, however, let me talk to him. I can't say that he was overjoyed to see me.

What does one say to a man one doesn't really know, a man who might not take kindly to sympathy or a well-meant offer of assistance?

"Hello, Marion. How are you?" That was a poor start. It was obvious how he was: embittered, disgusted, angry, hurt, resentful, - you name it.

"O.K., Doc." He was sitting on a cot, cradling his chin in his hands, looking glumly at the gray, cement floor.

"I hear you're in a bit of trouble." Another error. Understatement.

He sneered. "You don't say."

..."Is there anything I can do for you? Anything you need?"

He didn't even bother to answer.

"Do you have a lawyer?"

"What would I do with a damn stupid lawyer? He couldn't do anything."

Ordinarily, I'm a patient man but I was beginning to think that I was wasting my time. What the devil! I came to offer my help. If he doesn't want it, to hell with him.

But I couldn't leave. There was something so completely desolate about the man, something so lonesome and friendless, so just plain miserable that I was held there almost against my will. It was as though I was seeing a friend in great pain and though I couldn't cure him, I was unable to tear myself away from his suffering.

So I'll try again. "Is there anything I can do?"

"Yeah. Get me out of here."

Naturally he'd ask that.

"Sorry, old boy. It can't be done. I've already talked to the judge and he tells me it's impossible. Too many people after your hide. He also says that you were high when they brought you in. That right?"

That did it! Opened the valve to the boiler and the steam came shooting out. "Yes! That's right. How else can one face life these days? This stinking world has to be shaded somehow."

He stood up, walked angrily across the cell, back and forth, back and forth, feeding on his fury but, finally, he turned to stare between the steel crossbars of the little window and as he watched the setting sun, the anger appeared to fade to be replaced by a deep sadness.   .

"Here we are," he mused, still looking out the window, "people on this earth gouging and snapping at one another, fouling the air we need to breath, ruining the water the Lord's animals need to drink, sending our armies to kill in response to the thieving demands and machinations of politicians, shouting and clawing, spitting and hating, filling the air with obscenities and rocks and bricks and bullets, singing hate and love and debauchery - taking sex and bisexual relations with no thought to protection against disease and misery ---How can you stand it, day in, day out, without puking?"

Anger had returned but this was a different kind of anger, a deep, deep emotion, something he had obviously been nursing for years.

"I'll tell you how. You put blinders over your eyes. See only that which you enjoy. Ignore the unpleasant. And if anyone tends to upset your neat little apple cart, you pull all the stops trying to get that person out of the way, incarcerated somewhere so you won't have to look at him and listen to your conscience."

Ah,ha! So he's blaming me - us - for the predicament he's in. And he's bitter. Bitter as alum.

But there are two faces to every coin and I wasn't about to bear the blame for the thoughtlessness of others. "So," I shot back, "how have you been an improvement to the world? How are you different? What makes you think you can condemn people, working people, common people, people of my generation, my morals, my philosophy? Do you have something better? Some answer to the dilemma of humanity other than hiding behind rudeness and drugs?"

He continued to stand with the brilliant rays of the setting sun lighting his face and as I watched him, it came to me that maybe he or someone like him might someday have the answer. The thought surprised me.

"Look at you," I continued, "dodging all responsibility. I'm looking and what do I see? You don't even fight your own battles."

He shrugged and turned away from the window, away from me. "Sure. I get a skin full, now and then. So I discover this lovely little field of grass and I move in where I can pick a blossom when I need it, where it looks as if your kind might let me alone, where I can walk in the woods, absorb the color and movement of the earth by day and the heavens by night, where the noise and stink and dirt of the city can't befoul my nostrils," he whirled back at me and his eyes blazed with anger, "but I might have known you wouldn't allow it - your kind. You can't stand to see someone who isn't as miserable as you are."

It strained me to keep from shouting back at him, insult for insult, like two children shouting 'I can' - 'You can't - I can - You can't - - - but that wouldn't accomplish anything. I struggled to calm down, swallowing my resentment.

There was one question remaining to be asked: "Did you plant that field?"

He was still on fire. "You think I did. You've

already made up your stinking mind. If I said 'No, I didn't plant that field but I wish to hell I had,' you wouldn't believe me - you wouldn't even hear."

"If you didn't plant it, who did'?"

He deflated suddenly and his dejection was painful to see. "I have no idea. If I had - - ".

I could finish the sentence for him. If he had he wouldn't be in this cell. He would be free.

I wanted to believe him. I wanted to see him free. I wanted to be damn sure that we weren't demanding payment for murder from the wrong man. So, after a long pause, I admitted it: "If you aren't guilty, and I hope you aren't, then I for one don't like to see you moldering in this cell building hatred and bitterness. You should be out of here."

"But I wouldn't want to see you go right back

to the life you've been living. You should be tackling those things that you are so concerned about." I surprised myself by becoming downright emotional as I continued, "You can write. Write! You can speak. Speak! You could, with your talents, make people listen, make them see the world as you see it."

"You once recited a poem to me and it contained a message, an important message, but poetry won't do it. Its prose, the prose you've been using right now, to me, hard and clear, concise and honest, the kind that every man understands. That's what people will listen to." The more I talked, the more convinced I became. "You can inspire people to change."

"Horseshit!" But he was listening.

"It's true. Believe me, it's true. People like

310

me, what you call square, we see the inequities of our civilization as clearly as you do but we take the easy way. You said it: we turn our heads. But would we if someone could force us to look squarely at the problems and insist that we try to do something about them? Would we, if we had a dynamic, voluble, clearheaded leader? And that leader? - - - It could be you."

"Crap!"

"Absolutely. It could be you. Man! What a chance you might have with a clear vision and your gift of words. Don't you see? People need a leader. People, all the people, your kind and mine need someone in whom they can believe. Since King there's been no one. We're waiting. Why can't that someone be you?"

Then more slowly, "But you'd have to be

clear headed. No one, not even a junky, will truly believe a hop head."

He had turned his back to me but I wouldn't have that. I grabbed his shoulder and jerked him to face me.

"Man! Tell the truth. Get out of here. Stop hiding and feeling sorry for yourself. Stop sulking like some baby-faced, milk fed idiot! Make your destiny. Don't be a coward hiding behind drugs and self-pity. Get out of here and get to work. Do whatever needs to be done. Nobody will listen unless you talk so make them listen. Get to work! If the world is sick, find the cure man! Find the cure."

He stared at me for a long time, not saying a word, then he shook his head with a kind of hopelessness, shrugged, turned his back and walked away.

Is this what leaders are made of?

CHAPTER TWENTY THREE

Doc:

As I sometimes do, I stopped at the Coffee Shop on the way home for a final swig and a relaxing word with friends. It's a nice place, one of those small nooks with red checked tablecloths, a cheeky waitress, and a glad-to-see-you proprietor; therefore even though it's off the main drag it does a pretty good business especially at night. Almost always you can find a friend to talk to, someone willing to toss for the check, someone telling a joke or singing the blues and the talking or listening as the case may be seems to help clear up the muddy spots of the day leaving you with a good feeling as though living isn't all on the minus side.

This night was unusual in that the place was quiet. Toward the back, two couples were laughing over beers and wiener schnitzels; Rocky was the only other customer in the place. He was sitting at the counter hunched over a steaming cup of java and looking as unhappy as Gerty had looked all day.

"Howdy, lovebird," I said. Usually he grins at that; tonight, he gave me a dirty scowl. "Why are you so happy? Someone step on your sore corn?"

He looked sourer than ever. "Happy, hell!" He took a sip of coffee, burned his tongue, and swore. Looked like nothing was going right for him, nothing at all.

After giving me a cold shoulder for a long five minutes, he sighed and gave up. "Have you seen Gretchen today?"

315

"Sure. Haven't you?"

"No. She won't answer her phone."

Ah, ha. Trouble in paradise.

"How come? What happened?"

"None of your damned business."

But apparently he had to tell someone and I was available. "I expect the wedding's off."

"The hell it is!"

He nodded. One beer and he'd be crying in it.

"What makes you think so?"

"You know Saturday night - Saturday night we went to St. Louis. Going to be a big night. Reservations at the Frontenac, dinner and dancing. But I screwed up. Met some people I used to know, drank too much, and was a damn fool. She got mad, grabbed up her stuff, slammed out to the car, whizzed off, and left me there. I had to taxi back to the hotel and then I tried to find her by phone, couldn't so I asked the State Patrol to watch for her then I was so damned tired that I went to bed and so damned worried and mad I couldn't sleep! And now she won't speak to me!"

I'd never heard anything that struck me so funny but I didn't dare laugh.

He'd seen the glint in my eye, though. "You laugh and I'll knock the hell out of you!" And he meant it, I could tell.

"What are you going to do?"

"What can I do? She won't answer the phone, she won't talk to me in the office, she locked me out of her apartment - what can I do? Damn."

I've never been very handy with advice to the

317

lovelorn. I always figured that each man has to muddle through his own problems the best he can and I guessed that Rocky would have to handle this in his own way. I couldn't tell him how to get along with Gerty. I wasn't at all sure that I was going to be able to stand her in the office. And then the picture of her with her eyes red, her slip showing, her lips trembling, all this flashed through my mind. Poor children. Love, the most unfathomable disease of all. There's no cure, just sweet misery.

Change the subject. Get his mind on another channel. Maybe I can't cure him, but I might be able to help him forget how bad he feels.

"I've been at the jail talking to Clark. Do you honestly think he's guilty?"

"I don't know. Saturday night I was dead

certain of it. Today, at the inquest, I wasn't so sure. When I saw how the press was treating him and people were out for his guts I felt sorry for him. You have any ideas?"

"No. None except that I can't help thinking that he's a victim of circumstances. He certainly does have a gift of gab."

"Yeah. But he's so bitter."

"Wouldn't you be? In his circumstances wouldn't you be? What about his background? Has he been in trouble before?"

"No. I was surprised at that. He's clean as a new-shined window. And his background surprised me. He was raised in Chicago or, rather, in a fancy home along the North Shore of Lake Michigan, his father is a wealthy businessman (in Europe, right now, I understand), and he's a graduate of the

319

University of Missouri with a masters in science. He could just about write his own ticket if he wanted to."

"I can't see it," Rocky continued. "Why is he down here barefoot and dirty skinning full of hop with possibilities like his?" He considered for a minute. "Maybe his girl left him."

Well, now! This time I had to laugh! But Rocky was dead serious.

"Perhaps you're right. He's certainly disillusioned with society for some reason. Is his father sending an attorney?"

° "Yep. Some big gun from Chicago. Thought he could threaten me or if that wouldn't work, bribe me to let Clark run after he was picked up the other night."

"He phoned again this evening to say he'd be here in the morning but I doubt the judge will let him take the poor buzzard out. That would be mighty poor politics on the judge's part and he's sensitive along those lines. He's coming up for reelection in a couple of months."

My coffee was cold in the cup and I was getting sleepy. Besides, there didn't seem to be an answer to any of the questions buzzing around in my head - or Rocky's either for that matter.

Love is one illness that the patient has to cure for himself so I couldn't be of much use to Rocky. Clark's fate was a problem which might be handled later but for the moment it too was a hopeless task so I'm going home to bed. Maybe the wife can relax me.

But I didn't even get out the door.

"Hey, Doc. Your wife wants you on the phone."

"Hello. I'll be there in a minute." I started to hang up but I heard her shout:

"No! Go to Canody's apartment - Minda Smith's house. Minda just phoned and she says that Canody is unconscious. Someone apparently hit her with a book end."

Good Lord! What next?

"Canody's, Rocky," I shouted, as I sprinted out the door. And he didn't stop to ask questions.

Rocky:

I guess if Doc hadn't been called to Canody's apartment I might have stayed and mourned in the coffee shop all night.

I was glad to know that Gretchen got home safely but I wished she would speak to me. I couldn't even get to her to apologize. I had tried sending her flowers; she had returned them by slamming her door in the delivery boy's face. I'd tried to get Doc's wife to put in a good word for me but she told me off before banging the receiver on the hook. And apparently, from Doc's attitude, I won't get much help from him. He thinks it's funny.

But the scene at Canody's took my mind off my own troubles. What a mess -

CHAPTER TWENTY FOUR

Doc:

I remember dreaming when I was a little tyke that some day I'd go pell-mell down the street through stop signs, dodging traffic, in a fire-engine red car with JAMES T. FARLIN, M. D. emblazoned on the doors and everyone would stop to stare and they'd say "Look at him go!" There'd be a police escort with sirens blasting a warning for folks to watch out, all the kids would run to see what the commotion was about, little old ladies would scurry across the street and out of the way and I'd be just about the most important man in town. Boy, how I was going to enjoy that! But that's not the way it was. What with worrying about keeping up with the trooper and the possibility of failing to see some poor old dastard staggering drunkenly along the side of the road and whether everyone will hear the sirens and be able to get out of the way not to mention the anxious wondering what was waiting for me at the end of the line - well, I just didn't have time to regret that my car isn't red, my name wasn't printed anywhere except on the note at the bank and at that hour of the night kids and little old ladies weren't likely to be in a position to envy or be afraid of me. Seems to me that a kid's dreams shouldn't be shattered like that.

We screamed across town, Rocky leading and me pursuing, and scrambled to a stop in front of Mindy's house. It's the little yellow house at the west end of South Street, the one that's built all up and down instead of sideways. You know the one, narrow, tall, the one with the high porch along the front.

Rocky bounded up those steps like he was made of rubber and was holding the door open for me before I'd had time to pull my bag out of the back seat of my car. I puffed up the steps and through the front door and there was Mindy leaning over the upstairs banister and screaming down at me. Damn! More stairs! I cussed, tripped on the first step and fell up the next three, gathered my last ounce of energy and struggled up all two hundred, eighty-nine thousand steps, and walked into the most God-awful mess I've ever seen.

Canody must have put up a good battle! The drapes were torn off one window, one leg of the coffee table had been splintered and the whole thing lay cockle-wobbledy up against the sofa, chairs were upside down, everything breakable had been broken, and she lay in the middle of it with a nasty, bleeding gash just above the hairline, her nightgown torn to shreds, in what looked to me like an awfully uncomfortable position. She was unconscious, the breathing rapid and shallow and the pulse thready.

"I came home and found her here," Mindy was explaining, so excited that her voice was becoming shriller by the second. "I'd been to Missionary and when I came in, I hollered up the stairs to see if she would like to come down for a cup of tea before bedtime - we do that sometimes - and she didn't answer. So I put down my things, put the fire under the teakettle, and came up to see if she had heard me. And here she was. Gracious! A lady isn't safe in her own home these days." She was jabbering like the incoming tide.

"I had been warned. Yes, Sister Johnson warned me. She said that I was asking for trouble taking in a good for nothing slut like her," she paused and nodded at Canody, "but I like the girl. I felt sorry for her. Besides I was just doing my Christian duty." Her head was bobbing up and down emphatically. Reminded me of a yo-yo on a string.

I noticed that Rocky was sniffing the air and when he glanced questioningly at me, I nodded. I smelled it, too, the odor of burned gunpowder. He began to move around the room and Mindy turned to watch him.

"That's the bookend they done it with," she chattered, keeping an eye on it as he used his handkerchief to pick it up. "That's the one. See there? There's blood on it." She sounded downright triumphant.

Rocky gave her a dirty look and I could just hear him thinking, "I'll bet your fingerprints are all over it."

It was a dandy bookend and a murderous weapon. Black ebony it was, carved into a kind of surrealistic form that always leaves me cold and it must have been stuffed with lead. Rocky studied the heft of the thing, then stuck it, handkerchief and all, into his pocket. Mindy's greedy eyes saw it go.

I was tending to Canody and Rocky paid her no mind, but Mindy rattled on. "The poor girl didn't come home 'till late this afternoon and she was all upset when she came in. Poor thing! I wanted her to go to Missionary with me but she said no, she didn't feel like it. I hated to go off and leave her with her time about up and all but the lesson was from Ezekiel and I didn't want to miss it. Those lessons are so beneficial. Don't you think so? My, such an inspiration!"

She stopped to breathe which turned out to be a mistake because it gave Rocky a chance to wedge in. "Did she come home alone?"

She blinked at him. "Eh?"

"Did she come home alone this afternoon or did someone bring her?"

"Oh! Alone. I don't know. Yes, I guess so. Alone. She's always alone; I didn't see a soul with her. Alone, yes, but she was shaking and white as a sheet when she came in. Trembling."

"Had something frightened her?" Rocky was looking along the far wall, feeling along its surface with his fingertips and, when he found the bullet hole, he nodded to himself.

Mindy jabbered on. "I don't know. I asked her and she said not to worry about it, she was all right. I kept telling her that she ought not to go out there in the woods looking for Lord knows what. She had some fool notion that her husband was killed instead of dying like the inquest said he'd done and she was bound and determined to go nosing around 'till she found out for sure. Of course, some folks say that they weren't married, just living in sin, but I always like to believe good of people until I know different, don't you? The Bible says, "Judge not that ye be judged" and I try to remember that. Seems like, nowadays, people are in too big a hurry to find fault; no charity in our lives anymore." She shook her head. "No charity at all." Over and around her words the sound of the ambulance cut to us. None too soon.

Canody had opened her eyes, gave me a weak smile and was struggling to try to sit up then, suddenly, she folded her arms over her abdomen and groaned. Ah! So the first bit of business would be the birthing of the baby - - - and I certainly didn't want to have to deliver it in the middle of this mess with Mindy looking over my shoulder.

I hadn't discovered any broken bones. We'd have to check by x-ray later but for now there didn't seem to be anything of that nature to worry about. Canody's breathing and pulse had eased somewhat but I was feeling a hurry to get the show on the road before something unexpected happened. Besides, I needed to go to the can.

One more thing I noticed at the last minute before I turned to follow the stretcher down the stairs: Rocky had leaned over and was prying at the edge of the hot air register with his knife. The whole thing lifted up and he reached down into the pipe and came out holding what looked to be a dark green, over-sized brick. He was turning it over and over in his hands and it flaked a little as he moved it and I saw his lips form the word and I could almost hear him whisper, "Marijuana!"

Rocky:

Well, hello! Imagine finding that here, I thought. For some reason it hadn't occurred to me that Canody might be actively involved in those murders but now, suddenly, it seemed like things were beginning to slip into line. Pot? Cran's land? Canody Pederson's interest? Jake's murder? Marion Clark? If I'd known that Gablongo had been in town I'd have been dead sure that they were all connected. I'd have bet a year's salary that the pot I held in my hand had been cut in Cran's old house. Canody Pederson seemed to have plenty of money; where did she get it? Jake saw a field of yellow flowers and was killed for talking about them. Clark - well, in spite of the circumstantial evidence against him, he may have happened into this cartel by accident.

Obviously I was going to have a lot more investigating to do but now I thought I could see a path.

And I'd have been dead wrong.

CHAPTER TWENTY FIVE

Doc:

The baby turned out to be a squirmy little red haired chap, a good, strong, seven pounds of gooey squalling boy. Looking at him I could imagine his father cussing at the outrage of life when he was that age. He'd have been just as noisy, just as mad, and just as cute as this one. What a shame they grow up!

After the x-rays were taken and checked and I'd hemstitched the tear in Canody's head and we got her cleaned and comfortable, I began to relax a little. She was still in danger but from all indications, she was coming out of it. Time would tell.

I found Rocky sitting in the Doctor's lounge waiting for me, nursing a steaming java, looking into it as though there might be poison there. Kale had joined him and I couldn't tell whether the frowns on their faces were the result of puzzlement at this turn of affairs or the aftermath of an argument over whose bailiwick was being intruded upon. Technically, this would be Kale's case but he knew and I knew that the shortest way to keep Rocky out of it would be to push him off Blue Bluff.

Kale was showing more pep than Rocky and me. "How's she doing, Doc? Are we going to be able to talk to her after a while?"

What do you say to such a stupid question? I opened my tired yapper and answered as politely as I could, "Good heavens, man! Talk to her! She was unconscious. Now she is asleep dreaming of beautiful naked gods and sterile goddesses for all I know and wouldn't want to be interrupted. How can you talk to her? Let her be!"

My attitude surprised Kale, I guess. He looked like he'd swallowed a wriggling fish and couldn't tell exactly how to stop its sliding down. His chin had dropped as far as it'd go, his bottom plate was showing, and his eyes had taken on a kind of startled look like my outburst hadn't been exactly what he'd expected but he did a neat recovery and I had to admire the poor bastard. I hadn't any right to trounce on him like that and I felt kind of sheepish about it.

So I sighed and started over. "Not before tomorrow, Kale, if then. It depends on a lot of things: when she regains consciousness, how much shock develops, how she gets along -

337

lots of things. Remember, she's worn out and sore and miserable and if you guys don't let her alone and allow her to recover in peace, I'm going to clean up the floor with the pair of you." This was a mighty big brag for me, the shape I was in, but I crossed my fingers and prayed they wouldn't put me to the test.

"Should we put a guard on her door?"

"Not right now. I'm going to stay with her for a while. And it would be a very foolhardy man who'd try to get past the nurse's station and into her room at this time of night. There's not enough traffic around here to keep something like that from going unnoticed. If you insist, I'll call the station to send a deputy to take over before I leave."

"Good! And can we talk to her tomorrow?"

"No promises. And absolutely not until I've

cleared it for you. She's had a rough time, a bad concussion and she could suffer massive shock. We'll just have to wait and see."

"But - "

"No buts. That's it! People are going to leave that poor girl alone."

The hospital was quiet after they'd gone. All the hustle had tapered off and there was only the soft murmur of restlessness, misery, and service that goes on in any hospital during the quiet hours of the night. Now and then a baby cried or someone groaned or the bell at the nurses' station gave off a muted ding but on the whole it was peaceful there and clean smelling and comforting. It's a fine hospital and I'm proud to be on the staff. It gives me a good feeling, times like this, to know that I can be a part of the good that goes on there.

As I watched Canody, I began to let my mind wander over the past week reviewing the hair-raising happenings that I'd been a part of, happenings that had hit the newspapers all over the state, things that made the good people of Cantor Corners go indoors, lock up, and hide. And well they might, I thought. It was beginning to look as though any of us might be next on the list.

Had it been only a week ago that I'd been playing poker at John's? Only a week. And now Jake was dead, and Turner, and Canody had just had a lucky miss and E.L. had a heart attack, and Marion Clark was in jail, and Karen Kline as far as I knew was still holed up in her house scared as hell but too sentimental to move away from Jake's precious flower bed. Someone had been growing a field of pot on Cran's place, and Cran - Cran had to have been murdered. The death dovetailed too well with the other deaths to have been an accident. Where was it going to end? Who was next on the killer's list?

No one, absolutely no one, was going to make me believe that these were all just separate happenings. Uh, uh! These had to be connected. There must be a tie-in. No two or three or a dozen people had perpetrated this disaster. It's one person. It has to be. One person.

For most of the night, I sat beside Canody's bed and as the time passed I reviewed the facts, sifted them over in my mind, picked up a piece here, examined it more closely, then put it back to pick up another. I remembered the sight of things, the smell, the sound, the movement. I recalled my own reactions to events, sorting them out, trying to drain them of whatever bias or fears there might have been. My wife's opinions popped into mind, her words, her actions, her understanding and patient, quiet love. Then there was Gretchen and Rocky and the two together and then back to Rocky, his words, his lack of words, and as I placed these parts after examining them, I saw that they were beginning to make a dim pattern and as time passed that pattern became more exact then along about sunrise at just about the time that Canody opened her lovely eyes and recognized me and feasted her eyes on her son and held out loving arms to him and peacefully fell asleep holding him close, about that time was when I knew the answer. Just about then.

Rocky:

Anxiety about Gretchen - whether I'd lost her for good through my own stupidity - absolutely clogged my mind. I was going through my own personal hell. There was little will left for worry about solving these crimes - and you saw that, Doc. Thank God for you.

At first, when you finally confided your theory to me, I thought you were crazy but to tell the truth, my theory wasn't much more than a gut feeling. I simply couldn't fit your theory with mine. It wouldn't gel - and I didn't give a damn.

"You mean you don't care?" you sputtered. "You're going to let a little spat with Gretchen get in the way of your trying to find the killer of some of your friends? Could you face the people who elected you if you do that? Could you live with yourself?"

"Let me tell you something, boy," you warned. " Right now, you feel like life might as well end if you don't marry Gretchen - but it wouldn't. You're going to have to carry on and you're going to have to live with whatever decision you make right now. If you care more about your hurt feelings than you do about the families of these murdered men, then you've lost my vote."

Thanks, Doc.

CHAPTER TWENTY SIX

Doc:

It's surprising how much good a couple of hours sleep, a good hot shower, and a filling breakfast will accomplish. Possibly I was getting my second wind like they say but whatever it was, the day seemed bright and cheery and I felt strong as an ox. The wife just worries about me for no reason.

"You have anything doing tonight?" I asked her.

"No. I hope I'll have a chance to sleep for a change."

"Then how about making up a bunch of sandwiches? I think I'll ask the boys in for a little poker. I need some relaxation."

"Poker!" I'd expected her to get loud. Right

345

again. "Poker! After not having enough sleep in Lord knows when? You want poker? Are you out of your mind? Geez!"

I couldn't help grinning at her reaction but I wasn't going to let her talk me out of it. "How about the sandwiches?"

She could see that this was going to be one of my stubborn days so she shrugged, nodded, and dove into the dishes with a lot more clatter than usual.

"And I suppose you want cake and ice cream and Jello and turkey." Sarcastic as well as loud.

O.K. I'd play along. "Whatever you think, dear. Turkey's fine and we might forget the Jello and have fixings on the side, maybe a bit of chocolate cake and apple pie?"

She gave me a dirty look but I could see that

she was having a hard time keeping a smile out of her eyes.

"Ha! You'll settle for baloney and like it. Does John furnish sandwiches?"

"No," I answered, kissing her ear, "but the boys don't think he's quite as sweet as you are." That always does it.

Down town, people didn't know what to talk about first. There was so much gossip, so many tales floating around that they were just hitting the high spots willy-nilly, hitting there, then over here, then back yonder - and not getting one bit of it right.

But there were a few tidbits that I heard with interest.

Through the vent into the barbershop:

"Did you know they let Marion Clark out of

jail last night? And they say he's holding a press conference this morning. Ten o'clock, they say. Channel eight."

"They did? How come?"

"Some high-powered lawyer came down from up north somewhere and raised hell."

"How the devil could he afford help like that? He looks like he can't find enough cash to pay for his next meal."

"I don't know. He must have connections, though or they wouldn't be giving him any press conference."

In the waiting room in the office:

"--- and they say that someone has been cutting timber off the old Crannahan place. There's an old road leading off the highway and heading up into the hills behind Blue

Bluff where it runs along Hunter's Creek and they found lots of newly cut trees and someone's chain saw."

"That right? I wish I'd thought of going in there with a chain saw. Someone got some real good lumber."

"Did they find out who the saw belonged to?"

"Not that I know of. Probably the owner will just go down to the station and ask for it. There was no law against his cutting if he had permission."

And in the corner coffee shop:

"I told the wife that that was a gun shot and she argued about it. But I know a shot when I hear one. Along about nine o'clock or nine-fifteen or thereabouts. I was just beginning to think about going to bed."

"That must have been before Mindy got home."

"Yeah. I saw the preacher's car stop in front of her house a few minutes later and Mindy - she sure has a struggle getting out of a car. Her dress hikes clear up around her neck."

The man's wife chimed in with her two cents' worth: "And I was watching out the window and I said to him 'Yep! There's something funny going on,' and a couple of minutes later after Mindy went in some man slipped out and around the other side of the house. I couldn't see who it was. I've been telling Mindy that it was dangerous having that female bitch in the house."

And over the telephone:

"Doctor Farlin? Ronald Jones, here." Let's see. He's the state pathologist.

"Yes?"

"We tested the refuse your man, Ben Stover, sent in. It was about one-third pot and two-thirds weeds."

I nodded. It figures.

"I've notified the County Sheriff's office but I thought you'd like to know so you can work with him on it."

"Thanks, Mr. Jones. I appreciate that."

Well! So much for that.

And in Alderman's Drug Store:

"- - and, Doctor, after you left yesterday, Missus Pederson - Canody, that is - she kinda slumped down in her seat and began to look real bad so I asked her if she'd like to rest a few minutes in Mr. Alderman's office before going out in this heat and then I helped the poor woman back there and she laid down on the couch where Mr. Alderman sleeps now and then, and I asked her if she'd like me to call you but she said no, she'd be all right in a minute, and for me to go back and tend to the customers."

"Was she there very long?"

"I don't know exactly how long. In fact, I got busy and forgot about her. Later, I heard Mr. Alderman come in the back door and go in there and in a minute or two they came out together. I noticed especially because she was so pale and he was helping her along. He was going to give her a lift home but right then Mrs. Appleby came in and Mr. Alderman always waits on Mrs. Appleby himself. I could see that he was torn between trying to help Mrs. Pederson and keeping on the right side of

Mrs. Appleby and I do believe that he would have left Mrs. Appleby just standing there if Kale Riley hadn't come along to buy some cigars and he offered to give Mrs. Pederson a lift. Kale helped her out and Mr. Alderman went back into the pharmacy to fill Mrs. Appleby's prescription. Poor man, I hope he wasn't too sharp with her - Mrs. Appleby, I mean."

And from Gretchen:

"Rocky has called once and Kale twice to get an O.K. to talk to that woman."

"What did you tell them?"

"That you were out and I had no authority in the matter. Rocky can talk to her from now on for all I care," she finished with a contrary little swish of her tail. "She's just his kind."

"If either of them calls again, tell them that I

want to check her first and then I'll let them know. And call the hospital. Tell Sister to be sure that no one gets into her room 'till after I've been there. I'll see her as soon as I can."

And over Channel Eight:

Damned if Clark hadn't made a half-assed attempt to look decent. He'd had his hair trimmed and was all gussied up for the interview. He looked almost presentable.

The newscaster was egging him on trying to work up a sensational piece of news tape. "What are you going to do? Do you think you'll be let off the narcotics charge?"

"That remains to be seen. But I did not plant that field of marijuana and I think the authorities will be jarred when they realize that they had the wrong man. They let a murderer run loose while they were holding me. In my book, this is just another incident of unjust judging. I am an independent thinker, not one who can be influenced by public opinion."

He had been sitting at ease in his chair but now he straightened and tensed perceptibly. "I came down to these hills to get away from the stink of the city but there's a stink here too. This country looks like a beautiful, clean, sweet place to live - a place where people aren't gouging at one another, snapping and grabbing and clawing for the top of the totem pole, a place where a man might be willing to look for the good rather than for the rotten in his fellow man. But I was wrong. It's the same here as anywhere, no better, no worse."

Turning to speak directly and earnestly into the camera, he continued, "What this country

355

needs is a good douche. Clean it up internally. What does it matter, really, what the outer appearance is if the inner man is clean, wholesome, and good? After all, looks means nothing; the good of the man lies within."

The reporter - good, old country boy - looked shocked. And he wasn't given time to edge a word in.

"Selfishness and the grasp for power are roots of evil; selflessness, that's the answer. Selflessness and charity. Through charity, we may become brothers instead of enemies. The members of the human race should act for one another each working for the equality, for the comfort and peace of all men, all men. From our first breath, we should learn it. In our mother's milk, we should learn it."

Here, he dropped his eyes for a long moment

but the vibrating thread of communication between us - him sitting before the camera, and me sitting comfortably in my office - continued and when he raised his eyes to look again into the camera, his face shone with conviction. "The day is not yet," he continued, almost whispering, "but it will come! It will come!"

And at Canody's bedside:

- - "and he killed Cran, Doctor. I know he did!"

"O.K., Canody. We'll get him. Rest assured."

Rocky:

And those bits of conversation were just what you needed to back up your theory, weren't they, Doc?

As it turned out, the guy with the chain saw was stealing that timber; furthermore, the gossip was right. Marion Clark's attorney didn't waste much time getting him out of jail. We expected that but we surely didn't foresee a press conference. We were a bit nervous about it because we had no idea what he wanted to talk about. In fact, we thought he might be wanting to talk about us - - - and he wouldn't be very complimentary.

Your plans to host that poker game, Doc, surely put me on edge. With both Jake and Turner gone and the rest of us pretty well stressed out, anything could happen.

And you planned it that way, didn't you?

CHAPTER TWENTY SEVEN

Doc:

I was locking the office door getting ready to go home for the night when the barber hollered, "It's building up for a storm, Doc. Mark my words! It's been too damn hot and muggy all day. Not a whiff of breeze anywhere. Look at that flag!"

The Stars and Stripes was hanging like a bedraggled rag from the top of the pole, not a breath of air to ripple its edges. The sky was blue, typical of these last summer days, but now that I'd noticed, it was the sultry blue of heat and dust and pollen and smoke - bits of debris that are ordinarily carried away by the wind. The menace was almost tangible, an electricity that Ozarkians have learned from experience to watch with anxiety. True, September isn't usually the month for tornados - they come more in the spring, say April or May, but that doesn't guarantee that the possibility doesn't exist. I've seen them in January and in November, and now, could be, I might see one on the 18th of September. Damnation! I wonder how this will affect my poker game.

They came anyway; I should have known they would. They were more restless, less patient, more reckless with their money, but nothing less than lightening striking the table between us or wind snatching up the money would stop them for long. If that happened, though, there'd surely be a hullabaloo!

The weather didn't stop the wife, either. "If you insist on having that bunch of thieves out here, O.K. But I don't have to stick around to listen to them. I'm going to take Gretchen to the movies. She needs cheering up, Lord knows." Glaring at me accusingly, she continued, "You men are the most aggravating creatures on God's green earth!"

"What time will you be home?"

"Not 'till we're good and ready."

"Watch out for the storm. I don't want to have to scoop you out of a pile of rubble." For all her yapping, I kinda like the old girl. Wouldn't trade her in for two twenties for anything in the world.

E.L. was the first to arrive and he was looking pretty spry for a guy who was as sick as he was. He really shouldn't have been out but it was impossible to keep him away from a poker game. Besides, I guessed it wouldn't hurt him.

"I'm O.K.," he answered my question. "so long as I don't overdo. My wife wanted me to water the lawn this evening and I told her to go fly a kite. Water costs money! And it's going to rain! Besides, I'm going to stop all that strenuous exercise."

Yeah. I know him. The only exercise he's interested in is the motion required to pocket his billfold. "Uh --, who's going to play in Jake's place?" he continued.

"Kale. He tells me that he hasn't played in years, quit right after he got out of the service, but once he gets started he'll probably step right back into harness like the rest of us."

"I heard he was quite a player while he was in France. Got so good they put him out of the game. But I guess he's maybe lost his touch by now." But I suspected that E.L. had his reservations about that.

The weather was building up, all right. A bank of low lying black clouds was beginning to blot out the evening sky and as I watched it moving in, I noticed a nifty little sports car coming up the road. Now who the hell was that? Whoever it was was out of luck. No house calls this night. This was my night off. Absolutely!- - - But I might have known. It was Marion Clark.

"Hurry," I shouted, holding the screen door open. "You're too pretty tonight to get wet. - - - Where'd you get the little beauty?"

"The car? It's mine. I'd left it in Chicago and one of the old man's flunkies drove it down for me last night." He laughed. "Pretty? Yes, aren't I? I decided to follow your prescription. Still think it will work?"

"From the looks of you, it's worked wonders already. I saw you on T.V., by the way. That was quite a performance."

"Think it will do any good?"

"It's a start. Perhaps it will shock some into paying attention."

Rocky, Kale and John must have driven up at the same time; leastways they exploded through the back door together.

"Boy! It's sure beginning to look black out there," Rocky said as he pulled his chair up to the table. "Let's get started. If we get a twister, this game is likely to be cut short and I want to be sure to get my winnings first."

"The way you play," E.L. grunted, "the wind will probably sweep the pot right off into your lap."

So that's about how things stood when we gathered around the poker table.

The cards ran good; the stakes high. First one then the other of us raked in the pot, piles of white and red and blue chips, each chip representing value, each pile representing thirty, fifty, maybe seventy five, one hundred dollars. And the evening was young.

Outside, the Devil began showing off. Lightening streaked the sky and thunder ricocheted. Suddenly, rain slashed down; just as suddenly, it stopped, leaving the earth in a kind of panic of expectancy for the next onslaught. Pitchforks of lightening kept the sky in an uproar each flash followed by thunder as though a million lost souls were applauding. Explosions of wind were hurled around this way and that, not straight across the land but in fits, first north, then east, then south, then west, chasing the tails of the black, black clouds and churning them into even greater anger. And between the fits of wind and rain, the quiet pressed against the earth, hot, oppressive, frightening.

In the beginning, silver began to clang on the table along with the poker chips, the whole to be raked off at the turn of a card, the silver to disappear into some one's pocket until it was needed. As the evening progressed tens, twenties, fifties, hundred dollar bills – were thrown into the pot and snatched up. So it went. Excitement building among the six of us, tense, spine-tingling excitement.

As usual, a bottle or two appeared when we first sat down and it seemed to me as time passed that the more tense the game, the more liquor consumed. Even E.L. had a sip or two.

To my amazement, John was drinking more heavily than anyone else and this just added to the nervousness he'd been showing all evening. He was playing a mighty tense game, a 'winner takes all, loser goes to hell' kind of attitude. Satan grant that he be the winner.

Outside, the storm seethed; low pressure approached its climax. Inside, John finally growled, "Come on! Let's cut off this penny-ante stuff! Deal, damn it! Deal!"

Someone answered, "One big pot and I can go home."

"Home, hell! It's early yet. What do you say?"

And so it was agreed. The wife came in, set out the sandwiches, plugged in the coffee pot and disappeared. Not one of us saw her go. A sudden gust of wind blew the back door open and someone automatically got up to close it without disturbing the game.

The tension was straining, taunt, harsh in the room. "Seven card stud," Kale said, as he anted. I didn't miss his signal. It had come just as we planned.

"Come on, gimme some cards," E.L. growled.

"You stuff any more greenbacks into your pockets, you won't be able to lift your puny ass up off of that seat," laughed Rocky.

Kale dealt. Three cards around, two in the hole and one up.

"Ace bets," he said.

That was John. "One hundred bucks."

"That let's me out," groaned Kale.

"Me, too." That was E.L.

We all jumped when lightening crashed outside the window. "Won't be long," I thought.

In the hole, I held the nine and Queen of clubs, with the Club King up. I called.

Clark stayed in.

Rocky, too.

Fourth card around, face up. Mine was the Jack of clubs.

And the skies opened up and the rain came down bouncing off the window panes, rattling on the roof. No one paid attention.

"Ace bets," Kale said.

John had drawn the deuce of Clubs. "Five hundred."

The guys, huddled over the table, didn't turn

a hair.

And I hoped – prayed - that Kale could deliver. "Five hundred and raise it five." I'd asked for this. Too late to back out now.

Clark stayed with us.

Rocky groaned mightily and turned over.

John's turn. "Five hundred to me and I'll raise a thousand."

"I call," As I pulled out my check book and began to scribble.

"Too rich for my blood," Clark said as he turned his cards face down.

John's the Ace of spades.

"Aces high," Kale talked almost in a monotone.

The expression on John's face - something like a cat in a dairy. Gimlet eyed. Greedy. "Five thousand dollars." He flashed out his check book and scribbled the amount, his signature, and threw it in.

I couldn't keep from looking at Kale, for the life of me, I couldn't, and when I did, I caught just a hint of a nod, all the reassurance I needed. "Call. Raise it five," and I signed another check.

No hesitation from John. None at all. "Call. And raise, eight thousand."

It's a good thing they couldn't hear my heart hammering. "I call." Short breathed, I was, too.

Fourth card up. Mine, King of diamonds; when it fell I gave an almost inaudible sigh. John's, the five of hearts.

"Aces bet," Kale sang.

John was ready to pounce. "Ten thousand."

O.K., old boy, I told myself. Steady now! Let's see how good an actor you really are. Watch it. Be calm. "Called, and this house against your drug store." Beautiful! Perfect! And I was scared spitless.

The silence around the table was tangible like the moment between the time you see the bomb explode and the moment you hear the noise.

"You're called," John answered, immediately.

Kale dealt, expressionlessly. Seventh card. Down.

I tried to be nonchalant as I peeked at the card - next to impossible but I did it. Ah! Ten of clubs. I almost sighed again but stopped it in time.

Kale: "Aces high."

"Twenty thousand."

There was a pile of paper in the center of the table, little scraps but a life time of earnings. And John was staring at it, tensing to reach for it, itching to rake it to his breast. The naked expression of greed made the final bet easy for me.

"O.K., John. Let's make this interesting," I drawled the words. "I'll see your twenty and raise two hundred shares of IBM against your marijuana."

"You're called!" He threw his aces down, face up, four of them, and started to reach for the money and then - - - he knew! Thoughts ran over his face like lightening had been running over the sky. His left hand continued to pull in the pile of paper but his right reached for the gun, fast, smooth movement, almost graceful, and brought it up and pulled the trigger and the bullet which had been meant for me plowed through the muscle of Rocky's protecting arm and struck with a "plunk" into the ceiling.

And that was all the time John had. Kale had been waiting for just such a move, had been expecting it, but even then he was almost too late. He made a leaping dive at John, John's chair crashed backward, his head slammed the floor, and he went out like a light.

And no one had paid attention to the coming or the going of the whistle of wind that pushed the storm on its way nor to the steady, cleansing rain that followed.

Rocky:

I knew when I sat down at that table that something was going to happen. There was too much tension, the pressure too high. Even the weather was conspiring to bring on an explosion but when it came, I was almost too late.

Yes, Doc. You had given me your theory and I'd been skeptical. Of course, I was skeptical. According to you, the murderer was one of the most highly respected people in the city; furthermore, I thought, there was no motive. I'd as soon have accused you.

But Doc, believe me. Even though I thought you were wrong, I'd have checked out your theory if you had given me time. I have to think that eventually we would have found evidence enough to bring charges. Of course your way was faster and a whole lot more convincing. But the cost could have been too high. What a foolish move, Doc, to take a chance like that.

CHAPTER TWENTY NINE

Doc:

I've never seen anything like the way the wife appreciated me the next day. She gave me holy hell for taking the chance I took but later she stood over me like a mother hen with one chick, waiting on me, guarding me, touching me, kissing me. Don't get me wrong. I didn't complain. It's just that I must have been getting old; it was making me nervous.

And Gretchen was even worse with Rocky and he was nervous already. When he came through the front door she yelped, lunged at him barely missing his injured arm, threw her arms around his neck, kissed him, hugged him, draped herself protectively around him and there she stayed, crying and laughing all at the same time. Rocky - his face held a special, tender lovingness to it, a kind of release from anxiety, a wonder at the gift of her love, a coming on of great happiness. Made tears come to my eyes but then, I'm just a sentimental old fool.

Finally when he got the chance he turned to me. "How does it feel to be alive, you old goat?" He clapped me hard on my peeling back. "Some men will do anything for notoriety but I'd have sworn that you were notorious enough already. You sure got your sour puss in the papers today - right beside mine."

This was news to me. The wife and I had been pestered by reporters all morning. I'd told them that Rocky was the hero - after all, he had saved my stupid life - but some photographers had taken snaps anyway as we left the house. But how had they printed them in the news so soon? One thing I insisted on: If they're going to print me, I hope they'll print me pretty.

"How's the arm?" I asked. "Give you any trouble last night?"

"No more than I expected. After I started talking to John, I forgot all about it."

"What did he say?"

Rocky didn't speak for a moment. It was as though he was remembering the conversation with sorrow and regret. "I guess he was relieved to get the whole story off his chest."

I began to take the dressing off his arm and Gretchen, bless her pretty little heart, kept standing over him and getting in my way. I could see that she wasn't going to be much use to me that day.

We all waited for Rocky to continue but it was hard waiting. Finally, the wife couldn't stand the suspense. "Rocky, what did he say?"

"Who? Oh, John, you mean." (He knew damn well whom she meant.) "Poor bugger. I feel sorry for him."

"So do I but I'd feel a lot sorrier if he hadn't tried to shoot me," I snorted. "So what's his excuse?"

"You know how he gets when he's gambling? No sense at all. That caused it, that and his pride."

Surely Rocky didn't think he was going to drop the subject at that point. "How's that?" I pursued.

And, mumbling as though just talking to himself, Rocky continued, "No sense at all. Like he was last night." Then as he picked up the story the words came quick and easy.

"It was a year ago last spring during one of his trips to St. Louis that John went on a gambling spree. Just going to relax for a few days and have a good time, he told me. Someone had tagged him for a sucker and had given him a nod of entry into one of those members only, off-limits casinos - the joint that's owned by Gablongo. He had never been there; maybe the place would be lucky. Well, naturally, they fleeced him - but good. By the time they shut off his credit he had gone in the hole so far that if he'd sold everything he owned he'd have still been in debt for the rest of his life. So they took his little nest egg as down payment and gave him an easy way to pay off the debt. He was a pharmacist, wasn't he? Licensed to dispense drugs, right? So, he could dispense - to them."

"Oh, no! He groaned. He would be caught for sure."

"But then it appeared that his luck had changed. He copied signed prescriptions for narcotics - some even bearing your signature, Doc - filled and mailed or hand delivered them to names and addresses supplied by" Gablongo and got away with it. No questions, no investigation, nothing. He became so confident that when those thugs told him that they'd furnish the seed and he'd plant, harvest, manicure and deliver marijuana, he stewed and fretted and worried about it but finally decided that he could pull it off."

"He would however have to overcome one or two problems. First trouble was that he didn't dare plant the stuff on his own place because his neighbors live too close and tend to be a bit too nosy. Number two, most of his farm fronts the highway and can be seen by any passing motorist. So, what to do?"

"Then Cran's place came to mind. It seems that Cran had taken him down into the little valley on a hunting expedition and he realized that it couldn't be seen without plowing through a mile or two of brush and climbing that mountain, so he looked around for an entry other than the one that comes in from Cran's side and finally managed to clear out path enough to drive off the highway cut, down into the ditch, up the other bank and through the brush to the old road (the same track that Turner used to bring out the timber he'd cut) and from there it was easy. It stood to reason that Cran wouldn't be likely to discover it since he paid so little attention to the farm other than that part around his own house."

"Another thing we should remember: John's pride. You know how he was, always wanting to put up a great front and be the up-and-coming personality kid pharmacist. If Cran found out about it and spilled the beans, he'd lose his prideful reputation - to say nothing of his personal freedom while he paid his debt to society for sale of controlled substance."

"And, another thing we should remember, he wasn't nearly as afraid of Cran as he was of Gablongo."

"So, he took the gamble and again he was lucky. He'd done the planting, watched the crop grow, cut it and hauled it up the hill and into the house, where he spread it to dry, no one the wiser. Once it was hidden in the house, he felt that it was relatively safe, not likely to be spotted by some chance hunter or fisherman, so he could relax a bit but he still had nightmares about Cran running into it.

"All through that winter, he spent his nights in that house manicuring the marijuana and Gablongo or one of his boys got in the habit of picking it up at the store, a thousand kilos at a haul. He was just processing the last of the crop and congratulating himself on his good luck when Cran came nosing around to find out who was using the house. Well, naturally, Cran, being no fool and quite a reprobate in his day, recognized the stuff right off which made John mighty nervous to say the least."

"But Cran wasn't in any hurry. He sat down, propped his feet up and offered John a drink.

385

This brought on an inspiration: why not slip a Phenol or two into Cran's drinks, just enough to put him out of action for a spell? From then on, it was easy. Before Long, Cran passed out and John proceeded to finish his work, clean up his leavings, and prepare to clear out. Once the evidence was gone, he figured, Cran could holler his head off but who would believe him?"

"But Cran had stopped breathing. Knocking him out for a spell was one thing but killing him, that was something else altogether! What to do? When John's eye lit on the Phenol box and the bottle, he realized that the bottle would probably be recognized as having belonged to Cran so he simply planted the box and the bottle where they'd most likely be expected, and he very nearly got away with it."

"Now see there," the wife chimed in. "I told you he'd been murdered! I knew it all the time."

Rocky glared at her, shut off the words that had been on the way out and looked at Gerty. She had plunked her little bottom down beside him on the table and was holding his hand and looking at him with adoring eyes, the most admiring expression I've ever seen on a woman's face

Well, naturally, with so admiring an audience Rocky couldn't help telling his tale. He continued:

"February. It was February when Cran was killed and John figured that as soon as he'd made that last delivery he was finished and done with Gablongo - but he didn't know those cats. When they read about Cran's death, they put two and two together and made another beautiful lever for cooperation. All they had to do was threaten to leak what they suspected, and John would be up for murder."

"So it wasn't long before they sent a couple of strong-arm boys around to convince him that his bill wasn't paid in full and that he owed them another crop; furthermore, when they wanted narcotics, he'd better supply them. He'd cooperate - or else."

"He tried to argue with them - that's when he was laid up in bed for a couple of days with some cracked ribs and a knot on his noggin - but he caved in, planted the field, the one that Jake happened upon, and began sending packets of "medication" from the drug store through our local airport via Army Reserve helicopter deliveries to Whitman AFB"

Plain as day, I could see Jake, easy going, sitting reared back in that chair telling us about the doe and the pretty field he'd seen and John sitting right beside him staring at the cards he held in his hand. It's easy to think back, now, and figure out just what must have been going through his mind.

Rocky continued. "So there was Jake, threatening to let the cat out of the bag and John couldn't let him do it."

"He bawled when he was telling me about this last night but he said that he couldn't help himself. It was either Jake or him. So he hid and, sure enough, Jake came nosing around early the next morning and John shot him just as he was approaching the door. Realizing that he couldn't leave the body there,

389

he pushed it into the trunk of his car and dumped it off at the ferry. We found the marijuana blossoms which Jake had held in his hand in the blood stained trunk of John's car this morning."

My wife sighed. "Poor Karen! What will she do?"

Rocky shook his head. "I think Karen suspected something like this but she was afraid to tell. She was even afraid to talk to us or to come to town so she stayed out there alone with that rose garden to give her comfort." He paused for a moment. "Maybe, if some of you women would try to become better acquainted with her and encourage her to join some of the doings here in town, keep her busy, it might help her get over the shock. She'll go bugs if she continues to stay alone, looking at that garden and thinking about Jake."

The wife had the good sense to be embarrassed. "I've thought of that - been so busy - will call her -

Rocky went on with his story. "John didn't know it at the time but Turner had witnessed the whole thing. He'd been up to his old tricks stealing timber off of Cran's Land and he'd found the field so he was just as interested in Jake's tale about the doe at the edge of the field as John was. Well, naturally, next morning he was there, flue and all, in plenty of time to see John stuffing Jake's body into his car. And, right then, Turner figured he had it made for life. Here was a chance for an easy income if he played his cards right."

"But by the time Turner plowed through the

early morning dew-moistened weeds and made it back to town, his temperature had risen and he was feeling like hell so he came to you, Doc, then wandered on over to the drug store to have your prescription filled."

"John was fast becoming an old hand at getting rid of witnesses and he wasn't wasting any love on Turner so it was the easiest thing in the world when Turner tried to blackmail him to substitute cyanide for the antibiotic in one of those prescribed capsules. He figured that, sooner or later, Turner was bound to take that pill, sick as he appeared to be, and when he did, he'd be far away from the drug store and no one would connect him with Turner's death. More likely people would think as you did, Doc, that Turner had died of a reaction to the antibiotics."

Yes. I could see that now. John had simply emptied the penicillin capsule, filled it with cyanide and thrown it in with the other capsules. Trouble was, up until I sat beside Canody's bedside in the hospital reviewing the facts one by one, I'd been concentrating on Jake's murder. Maybe, just maybe, if I'd connected Cran's death with Turner's a bit sooner, I'd have been able to prevent Canody's injuries.

"And all this time Canody had been searching for some explanation to Cran's death but not found a thing. It wasn't until she saw John with Gablongo that she began to suspect him. Remember, she knew Gablongo and his rackets. She pulled a fainting act while John was out of the store, was helped into his office and had a chance to

393

search the place before John found her there. John confessed to me that he'd been holding out a kilo or two at a time from delivery to Gablongo. It would make a pretty fair income once he was tucked away in some foreign country. But Canody found it, took one, hid it in her purse and when John missed it, he knew he had to kill her, too."

Thank the dear Lord for Mrs. Appleby. If she hadn't come along just when she did and stopped John from taxiing Canody home, Canody wouldn't have had a chance.

"Rocky continued. "So he went to her room that evening and tried to shoot her, shot once and missed, and then she jumped him and fought like a tiger. He lost the gun in the scuffle - had to grab the bookend and whack her with that. Then he picked up the gun, pointed it at her but he couldn't do it. And what the hell! She looked dead already. Why arouse the neighbors with any more noise than necessary? So he pocketed the weapon and started searching for that kilo of pot. And he almost got caught. Mindy came home and he had to beat it while she was in the kitchen putting the fire under the teapot."

Rocky turned to me. "How did you figure it out, Doc? You knew, didn't you?"'

Yes, I knew - or hoped I did. If I'd been wrong, my bluff certainly would have been expensive. Damn! I could have lost our home, our savings, everything. "Yep," I answered, "it was the poison. When I finally cottoned onto the fact that both Cran and Turner had been poisoned, I asked myself, 'Who had access? And the knowledge?' Well, John! Of course! It had to be John."

"The motive? When I saw Canody's reaction to Gablongo there in the drug store and when you found the kilo in her room, I put two and two together and decided that John, Canody and Gablongo were in cahoots in a dope ring. It was hard to swallow - I'll admit that - but the circumstances seemed to point squarely in that direction."

"Then Canody was attacked and I knew I was wrong; she wasn't in on it at all. But John was. He had to be. The state lab had reported marijuana in that stopped up drain behind the drug store, John's nervousness, the deaths by poison, - - - everything pointed at him."

"If I was right, if his records proved to be as jiggered as I suspected they were, he could be put away on a narcotics charge but that wouldn't make him pay for murder. In my opinion, he needed to be put out of circulation immediately and forever. But how?"

I shuddered, thinking of that gun blasting off in our kitchen. Good heavens! What a chance I'd been taking.

We sat there, silent, for a moment with a kind of final, wordless, thankfulness to God for watching over us, for allowing us a hunch here and there, for protecting us in the clinches.

And your mother, boys, and my wife - I guess they were giving thanks that their men were still alive. Gretchen tenderly raised Rocky's hand to her lips and kissed it, his eyes following her movement like a caress; the wife scooted closer to me and put her hand on my shoulder with a gentle squeeze. It felt good to be alive!

Rocky:

Doc didn't tell you about the melee following the shooting. John was spread out on the floor, cold as a mackerel, Kale sat astraddle of him, I was dripping blood, E.L. was pocketing his money, Marion Clark had assumed a black belt position, and Doc stood up, gathered the cards, put them neatly into the box then picked up the phone, dialed, and said to the cop on duty, "Come out to Doc Farlin's house and bring an ambulance." And then, "Come on, Rocky. Let's go see about that arm."

Right about then, his wife came bursting in

with fire in her eye. "Can't you scoundrels play cards without tearing up my kitchen?", then, seeing John, she squealed, "What happened?" Followed by, "Rocky? Is that blood?"

Doc brushed past her, grabbed my good arm, picked up his emergency kit as we strode through the parlor, led me into the bathroom and instead of unbuttoning my sleeve, picked up a pair of scissors and cut the damn thing off.

Don't ever let anyone try to tell you that a gunshot wound isn't painful. I know better. I tried to hold still while he cleaned and wrapped my arm to his satisfaction but he saw me grimace so he insisted that I take a pain killer. I took it rather than take time to argue. After all, I was missing all the action. The kitchen, that's where the action was.

I needn't have worried. Kale had taken over, the cops had come and the EMT's carted John off to the hospital. Doc's wife made some coffee and E.L., Clark, Doc, his wife and I collapsed - but not for long. My pain killer began to take effect so Doc shoved me out the door with instructions to Gerty to drive me home and put me to bed. I don't even remember the ride.

Thank God for one thing! Gretchen wasn't mad at me any more. As Doc said, she jumped into my arms and stayed there. He had to pry her loose to remove my bandage.

With Gretchen so near, with her looking at me like that, it was hard to sit in Doc's office to bring him up to date but I figured that I owed him one for helping to solve a difficult case, for being there when I needed him and - - - for Gretchen.

EPILOGUE

Doc:

"So, boys. Those were exciting days. Your dad was one hell of a Sheriff and your mom, our Gretchen, was - is - mighty special. I know you are proud of them and you should be."

Wistfully, he added, "One of these days, maybe they will move back to these Ozarks. Maybe they will move home."

The fire had died, moonlight shone like a slash on the river, dry leaves rustled slightly. The boys watched, mesmerized, as the old man took his hands out of his pockets, grasped the arms of the camp chair, shoved himself out of it and stepped toward his camper.

Then he stopped, turned back and said,

slowly, "It's ironic, isn't it, that today in some states the only thing you need to do to buy pot legally is to whine about some pain or other and buy it in a drug store. Three of my friends died to keep that from happening. Doesn't seem right somehow. But I'm just an old fuddy-duddy. Who am I to say that knocking your brain all to hell by using drugs should be off limits to the human race?"

He paused, scratched his chin, looked up, shrugged and grinned, "But there is something good, I suspect, in everything God put on this earth and maybe today's scientists have found a good reason for raising marijuana. I have my doubts - but who am I to judge?"

The three men stared at this old, bent man, this octogenarian who had devoted his life to service to others, this man who would fight for his friends, whose zest for life included his fight to live by his own rules and the guts to fight for freedom and honesty and trust.

Doc winked then turned toward his camper but Rocky stopped him with a bear hug

"Do you remember?" he asked Doc with a grin, " as Gretchen and I were leaving your office that morning, you groaned, then grinned and said "Well, back to work. I just now took a peek into the reception room and there sits Reuben Frye. Poor old bastard. Every time he gets a small fart lodged sideways, he gets all nervous and upset."

Red Rock rang with their laughter.

ISBN 142515221-X